Lois Lenski's

CHRISTMAS STORIES

Other Books by Lois Lenski

Historical

Phebe Fairchild, Her Book
A-Going to the Westward
Bound Girl of Cobble Hill
Ocean-Born Mary
Indian Captive
Blueberry Corners
Puritan Adventure

Regional

Bayou Suzette
Strawberry Girl
Blue Ridge Billy
Judy's Journey
Boom Town Boy
Cotton in My Sack
Texas Tomboy
Prairie School
Mama Hattie's Girl
Corn-Farm Boy
San Francisco Boy
Flood Friday
Houseboat Girl
Coal Camp Girl
Shoo-Fly Girl
To Be a Logger
Deer Valley Girl

LOIS LENSKI'S
CHRISTMAS STORIES

Written and Illustrated by

LOIS LENSKI

J. B. LIPPINCOTT COMPANY

Philadelphia   *New York*

AT

Day of Work and No Cheer from PURITAN ADVENTURE, copyright, 1944, by Lois Lenski.

How Christmas Came to Blueberry Corners from BLUEBERRY CORNERS, Copyright, 1940, by Lois Lenski.

The Pink China Bonbon Dish from THE CHRISTMAS ANNUAL, 1939, Copyright renewed, © 1966, by Lois Lenski.

The Uninvited Guest from COTTON IN MY SACK, copyright, 1949, by Lois Lenski.

Kayla's Christmas from BERRIES IN THE SCOOP, copyright ©, 1956, by Lois Lenski.

The Christmas Program from PRAIRIE SCHOOL, copyright, 1951, by Lois Lenski.

La Christine Comes from BAYOU SUZETTE, copyright, 1943, by Lois Lenski.

Before Snow Flies and *The First Star* from WE LIVE IN THE NORTH, copyright © 1965 by Lois Lenski.

The Angels' Song, A Greater King Than They, Shepherd, Lonely Shepherd, and *O Babe in the Manger* are from WE ARE THY CHILDREN, copyright, 1952, by Lois Lenski. Published by Thomas Y. Crowell.

No Room at the Inn, Wake Up, Now, Long Will We Remember, and *It's All We Have to Give* are from THE LIFE I LIVE, copyright © 1965 by Lois Lenski. Published by Henry Z. Walck, Inc.

SOURCES OF STORIES

Day of Work and No Cheer was first published as a short story in THE SHINING TREE AND OTHER CHRISTMAS STORIES, Alfred A. Knopf, Inc., New York, 1940. It became Chapter V in PURITAN ADVENTURE, J.B. Lippincott Company., New York, 1944.

How Christmas Came to Blueberry Corners was first published as a short story in THE CHRISTMAS ANNUAL, Augsburg Publishing House, Minneapolis, Minn., 1937. It became Chapter XII of BLUEBERRY CORNERS, J.B. Lippincott Company., New York, 1940

The Pink China Bonbon Dish was first published in THE CHRISTMAS ANNUAL, Augsburg Publishing House, Minneapolis, Minn., 1939; copyright renewed in author's name, 1966.

The Uninvited Guest, from COTTON IN MY SACK, Chapter IV. Lois Lenski, 1949.

Kayla's Christmas, from BERRIES IN THE SCOOP, Chapter VII. Lois Lenski, 1956.

The Christmas Program, from PRAIRIE SCHOOL, Chapter IV and pp. 82–84. Lois Lenski, 1951.

La Christine Comes, from BAYOU SUZETTE, Chapter IX. Lois Lenski, 1943.

Before Snow Flies, from *Christmas Tree Farm* in WE LIVE IN THE NORTH, Chapters III and IV. Lois Lenski, 1965.

The First Star, from *Auto-Worker's Son* in WE LIVE IN THE NORTH, pp. 67–69. Lois Lenski, 1965.

Two Stories, *Christmas on MacDonald Street* and *The Christmas Fake*, the play, *Visit of the Shepherds*, and all the poems have not been previously published. They appear here for the first time, with the exception of the poems in *Visit of the Shepherds*, from WE ARE THY CHILDREN, Lois Lenski, 1952, Thomas Y. Crowell, and THE LIFE I LIVE, Lois Lenski, 1965, Henry Z. Walck, Inc.

CONTENTS

POEMS

Foreword

Christmas has been celebrated in many ways around the world. There are as many ways of celebrating Christmas as there are people and traditions and Christian customs. Each group adds something to it of enrichment or beauty; or subtracts part of the essence of its meaning. Despite the cheapness and commercialism which has changed it in modern times from an essentially religious festival, it still retains its vital and universal appeal. Those cynics who discount it are themselves the losers. For in this rapidly changing world, its message of goodwill is still, as it has been since the birth in Bethlehem, the one thing the world needs most.

Christmas in America has taken many forms. It has definitely been colored by contributions from national European groups, some of whom have retained their Old World customs intact, others of whom have allowed them to be infiltrated by an "American" spirit. Our Christmas customs have been affected, too, by our many forms of religion, which are as varied as our cosmopolitan inhabitants. Climate, and also the occupations of people controlled by their environment, has brought about variations, with the result that we have many kinds of regional Christmases. Some of these are described in this book.

There are always on the sidelines, of course, children who do not know Christmas and have never experienced it. That they instinctively reach out toward this unknown symbol of beauty, once given an opportunity, makes it all the more important that they not be overlooked. One of the best ways to fight evil is to spread beauty.

Lois Lenski

EARLY CHRISTMASES

A Day for Gladness

Oh, not a day for toiling,
And not a day for work;
Unlike all other daytimes
When man must never shirk.

Oh, not a day for weaving
Or tending cooking pot;
This day, of all time's passing,
Such things must be forgot.

Oh, not a day for shadows,
For weeping and for grief;
And not a day for jailing
A scoundrel or a thief.

Oh, not a day for scolding
The child who breaks in song,
Who runs instead of walking,
Unconscious of a wrong.

Today a day for gladness,
For happiness and mirth;
A day made for rejoicing,
For 'tis the Christ child's birth.

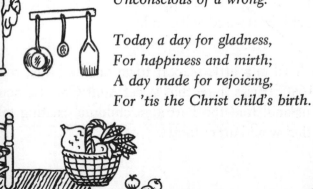
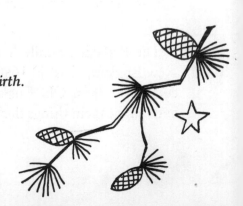

DAY OF WORK AND NO CHEER

A Puritan Christmas

BEFORE the first settlers came to our shores, Christmas was a celebration of joyous and merry exuberance in Old England. Because it often ended in drunkenness and disorderliness, the Puritans frowned upon it, and when they came here decided to leave it and the celebration of all other saints' days behind. They who themselves had lived as boys and girls in this freer "merrier" England, in the interest of freedom of thought and worship, took upon themselves the garments of austerity and harshness. They banned the very pleasures they had most enjoyed. As newcomers to a promised land, the Puritans instituted Thanksgiving Day and Election Day to take the place of Christmas and saints' days.

That first generation of Puritans must still have remembered the joys of the Christmases of their childhood; and at least one of them, a fictitious "Aunt Charity" might have shown the repressed little Puritan children, who were never allowed to go "singing, whistling, hollering, or running along the street," what an Old World Christmas meant. The excitement that it caused is told in *Day of Work and No Cheer*.

Forbidden, forgotten, banned, and disapproved of for many years, Christmas did not die. It still lives—and will ever live.

The Partridge family lived in a little seaport town on the bleak, rocky New England coast in 1640. It was there that sweet Aunt Charity, newly come over from Old England, told the Partridge children exciting tales and taught them things they would never forget.

3

"What? Not keep Christmas?" asked Aunt Charity. "As I'm a God-fearing woman, what's this new world a-coming to?"

"No, we keep it not," said Goodwife Partridge sadly. "Life has been hard with us these ten years. It hath taken all our time and strength to feed and clothe our bodies—we've had none left for jollity."

"So sad-faced and dour you've all become!" Charity went on. "The moment I stepped ashore I thought you must all be a-mourning for summat, your countenances looked so heavy and sad. The childer—haven't they . . ."

Goodwife Partridge looked about at the little faces. She shook her head sadly as she spoke: "Seaborn was born on the ocean and the others here in this country. They know not the meaning of the word Christmas. The Governor, the Parson, and the Magistrate say 'tis wrong. They say we came here for work and not for jollity."

" 'Tis time you heard it then, childer sweet!" laughed Aunt Charity. "Your Aunt hath come over the ocean to tell you of Christmas, sweet Christmas!"

"Oh, tell us, do tell us, Aunt!" begged the eager children.

"When thou hast been here for ten long years, thou wilt no longer laugh and tell merry tales," said Goodwife Partridge in a low voice.

" 'Tis time you heard of life in Old England, where mirth and jollity still reign, where life is not so stern—Dear Lord, may I never forget, no matter how old I grow. When the Christmas time comes in Old England, dear-my-loves, 'tis the time when Jack Frost takes us all by the nose, so we make shift to rub out winter's cold by the fireside. 'Tis then the great Yule log is put in the fire, stories are told and songs are sung. And all the little boys and girls have puddings with raisins in them and minced pyes and Yule cakes rich and sweet . . ."

"But is it not wicked, Aunt?" asked Seaborn, pondering thoughtfully. "Parson Humphrey would say that such things are an abomination of heathendom and the ruination of souls."

"But oh, what fun!" cried Comfort, her eyes sparkling. "I should have liked it, had I been there."

Aunt Charity sat down on the bench before the fireplace and the children crowded close. It was a short time, but three months only, since this wondrous aunt had come over from Old England with strange words in her mouth, strange words which were ever a temptation to hear. In the short time she had been here, the children had learned to love her dearly. Such tales as hers had never met their ears before nor set their hearts so eagerly fluttering.

"First of all the pewter and brass is polished so bright, it shineth like the sun indoors!" Aunt Charity's sweet voice went on. "The servants are washed and dressed in prettiest bib and tucker and here and there they run, as smug as new-licked puppies. For into the Great Hall all the Master's tenants and neighbors soon foregather to drink of his good ale, into which toasted Yule cakes are soaked and softened. The Yule candles are already alight when the mummers come to shout:

> " 'A Merry Christmas and a Happy New Year,
>   Your pockets full of money and your cellar full of cheer!' "

"Sister!" interrupted Goodwife Partridge severely. "Why remind us all

of things which have gone past, never more to return? Dost wish to breed discontent? Here we have more solemn things to engage the mind—work, the shortness of life, the swift coming of death. I want not the children's heads befuddled. See how bright their eyes do shine, like in a feverish sickness, when one lieth at death's door!"

"Hush! Speak not of death!" Aunt Charity looked down at the children. "They are alive for the first time in years. 'Tis the first happiness they have known. The mere telling doth give them pleasure, their little lives have been so dark and drab, so starved . . . Yes, ye have spent time and strength to feed and clothe their bodies, but their spirits ye have forgot."

She went on with her story: "The bouncing log on the chimney hearth doth glow like the cheeks of a country milkmaid. All the spits are sparkling, for the Hackin—a great sausage must be boiled by daybreak . . ."

Gaffer Partridge suddenly entered the low-ceiled room. "*Hackin! Hackin!*" he cried sternly. "Who speaks of Hackin here?"

"I tell the sweet childer of Christmas time in Old England, John!" answered Charity quietly.

"Christmas time in Old England!" exclaimed Gaffer Partridge. "Is there still such a thing? I had forgot. I had forgot. Christmas! To think it still goes on as it did when I was young and ran about in pinafores. Here we have no time or place for such goings-on, but it can do no harm for the childer to know what once it was."

"Husband!" cried Goodwife Partridge in alarm. "Hast lost thy wits? How canst thou see thy children's heads befuddled by wild tales?"

Gaffer Partridge seemed not to hear his wife's words. He sank down heavily on the settle and stared into the fire. He spoke as if to himself alone: "I came but now from the village green. There saw I Goody Nichols chained to a post for scolding her man in a loud, harsh voice. William Muddleton was set in the pillory for idleness; and at the whipping post yonder, Constable Cartwright laid the cat-o'-nine-tails on a poor wretch's back, the while his cries did rend the air. Here in this fair land we seem to think of naught else but wrong-doing. I like it not. Mirth and jollity we have forgotten quite. Is this the good life we came so far to find?"

"Oh, Father!" cried the lass Comfort, running to his knee. "Did you keep Christmas, too, when you were young like me?"

Gaffer Partridge turned away his head. The tears rolled down his cheeks one by one.

At daybreak on the twenty-fifth of December, two days later, no sound of caroling or of chimes broke the morning quiet. Now and then a chill breeze blew inward from the sea, bringing scattering gusts of snow. One by one the chimneys of the thatch-roofed cottages began to shown thin trails of smoke.

Without, in the harbor, the frail ship *Fearless* still rocked at anchor. Salt fish, clapboard, and furs to a sufficient amount had not been assembled for her cargo, and the early closing-in of winter had prevented her return voyage across the Atlantic.

Through the narrow, winding path, on which a few months before the town cows had made their slow and patient way to pasture, walked Comfort Partridge with hood and shawl wrapped tight about her head and shoulders. In her cold, unmittened hand she carried a pail half-filled with fresh, froth-covered milk. As she hastened along toward her home, her little cowhide shoes made a sharp patter on the hard, frostbitten ground. Suddenly she stood still and bent her ear to listen.

The Town Crier, stoop-shouldered and frowning, stepped round the corner. He rang his bell noisily, then in the pause which followed, cried out: "No Christmas! No Christmas!"

Christmas! All of Aunt Charity's words came tumbling back into the child's mind. She stood still and thoughtful, scarce heeding the little group of people who gathered to hear the Crier's words:

"Work to go on as usual . . . brick-making, blacksmithing, the chopping, riving, and sawing of wood . . . Townsmen to raise the new dwellings . . . Women to spin in their doorways where they may be seen. A day of work and no cheer . . . a day of work and no cheer . . . by order of the Governor of the colony . . . to be enforced by the Magistrates . . ."

The listening people tightened their lips and went their way. Comfort shivered with the cold. A tear rolled slowly down her cheek. She grasped her pail more tightly and hastened home.

The heavy batten door swung slowly shut behind her. She put down her pail, removed her shawl and hung it on a wooden peg. Then she approached the table where the family waited—her parents and aunt seated on wooden stools and the children standing.

"Thou'rt late, Daughter!" reproved Goodwife Partridge. "What delayed thee?"

"I stood for a moment . . . to listen to the Crier, ma'am," answered Comfort. She pressed her white coif more firmly over her wayward curls, then straightened her white kerchief and apron. "The Crier said . . ." her voice pierced the silence, " 'at Christmas is a day of work and no cheer." Her blue lips trembled.

"And so 'tis!" echoed her mother. Then more sharply, "Hast forgot thy message? Didst inquire about Neighbor Minching and his sick wife? She's better—Goodwife Minching?"

Comfort Partridge shifted from one foot to the other. She was a responsible child. She had not lived her eight years in vain—eight years spent in learning not to forget.

"No, ma'am, I forgot not," she replied slowly. "Goodwife Minching's taken a turn for the worse and Endurance is come down with the sickness, too. And the cow is 'most dry. This—'tis all the milk could be spared. Neighbor Minching asked if you and Aunt Charity could come and care for the goodwife, since Endurance must also keep to her bed."

" 'In the midst of life we are in death!' " Goodwife Partridge gave her sister a meaningful look.

As soon as the porridge was eaten and the table board cleared, the two women left the house for their neighbor's. No one in the little seaport town ever called on a neighbor in vain. Then Gaffer Partridge left, too, to help with the raising of a new pine cottage, one of those being built for the newcomers from the *Fearless*. And so the children were left alone.

It was when Comfort and Thankful were scrubbing the table board that they remembered.

"Just so do they do in Old England to make ready for the Christmas feast," said Comfort thoughtfully. "Aunt Charity said the board is always scrubbed till it shines as white as new-fallen snow."

"I wish we lived in Old England," said Thankful, biting her little red lip.

" 'Tis here we can worship God as we please," said Seaborn seriously. Being the eldest and a boy, he felt heavy upon his shoulders the responsibility of the younger ones. " 'Twas for that our parents came."

It seemed strange to hear the sound of children's voices. When their elders were present, they knew well to hold their peace and listen respectfully, speaking only when spoken to. Only when the elders were absent did their bright voices rise and fall freely like the piping of happy birds.

"I've seen laurel and ground-pine and hemlock greens a-growing in the woods," cried little Waitstill. "We need not go to Old England for them. They grow right here, even as our fuel grows at our very doors. We could fill our arms to overflowing . . ."

"Why, so we could, my lambie!" answered Comfort, her eyes suddenly aglow. "Seaborn, let us keep Christmas just for ourselves this day— while the elders are away. 'Twill be a little play of our own and can do no harm. I mind all the things sweet Aunt Charity did tell."

Seaborn shook his head. "Parson Humphrey saith such things are an abomination . . ."

The door opened and Aunt Charity walked in.

"Your mother can do all that's needful for Goodwife Minching and her daughter," she announced. "She was worried for fear God-be-thanked might fall in the fire and be burned or you'd forget to fetch wood enough and let the fire go out, so I thought best to return."

"Oh, Aunt Charity!" cried Comfort eagerly. "How good of you to come! We thought to keep Christmas this day, whether the Magistrate says so or no . . . just for ourselves at home . . ."

"Christmas! Good Yule!" said Aunt Charity softly. "I never thought I'd live to see it in this hard, cold, righteous land—but mayhap I will."

"There's Silence Pitkin—she's always sad and never talks or smiles," ventured Thankful timidly. "She would like Christmas, I know full well."

"And Preserved Rogers," added Waitstill. "He never plays stoolball for fear the Magistrate might pass and see him."

"And Temperance Seward," added Comfort, speaking more boldly now, "who always talks of death and thinks each day her last. We'll make things ready—the Yule log, a great feast, the Christmas greens—and bid them all welcome!"

"None of the other children know about Christmas," said Thankful shyly. "They have no sweet Aunt Charity to tell them."

" 'Tis time they knew," said her aunt. Her words were short, but a smile played on her lips. She set to work with a will and the children scurried about and helped.

"But what if the Magistrate comes?" asked Seaborn.

At midday, when sad-faced Silence Pitkin and timid Preserved Rogers and solemn Temperance Seward and other little boys and girls came to the Partridge home, they saw many suprising things. They saw Christmas greens, laurel, hemlock, and ground-pine wreathing the batten door and embowering the fireplace. They all helped drag the Yule log in to the hearth, the girls first washing their hands at Aunt Charity's behest, in order, according to the old belief, to make the fire burn more brightly. They saw the shining board set with a feast and they ate heartily thereof— roast pork and codfish and mackerel, besides pumpkin sauce, beans, and parsnips, and honey and maple sugar for sweets.

Afterwards came the games, *Blind Man's Buff, Puss in Corner, Hot Cockles, Forfeits, Shoeing the Wild Mare,* and *Hoop and Hide.* Charity taught them all and none was slow in learning except little God-be-thanked who managed always to get in the way of the others, and Silence Pitkin who had sometimes to sit down for lack of breath, so unaccustomed was she to the playing of games.

Then Aunt Charity taught them a lusty carol and they all sang it together:

> *"Lo, now is come the joyful'st feast!*
> *Let every man be jolly,*
> *Each room with ivy leaves is drest,*
> *And every post with holly.*
>
> *Now all our neighbors' chimneys smoke,*
> *And Christmas blocks are burning;*
> *Their ovens they with baked meats choke,*
> *And all their spits are turning.*
>
> *Without the door let sorrow lie,*
> *And if, for cold, it hap to die,*
> *We'll bury't in a Christmas pye,*
> *And evermore be merry!"*

As the little voices rang out happily, Comfort noticed that her father and mother had returned and were standing back in the shadows watching. Then Preserved Rogers saw his parents and Silence Pitkin hers and before any one realized what had happened, the Partridge house was filled to overflowing with neighbors. The carol was sung over and over again and all the people smiled as they listened.

Suddenly a loud knock was heard at the batten door. The song died away and the children ran to their parents.

"What meaneth this frumpery?" a man's voice sounded in loud, cruel tones. Everyone knew it was the Magistrate. His face was dark and flushed with anger as into the low-ceiled room he strode.

"What meaneth this?" he cried, pointing with his wooden cane. "What mean these greens about this hearth encircled?"

Little Waitstill had not lived long enough—but five years only—to learn that man can change a beautiful world into a sour one of his own making. In his innocence, he thought the strange, dark man had come not to berate, but to admire. He clapped his hands eagerly.

"Oh, good sir!" he cried. "We found all the greens a-growing at our very doors. Dost not rejoice to see them? It seemeth as if the summer's sun hath changed the earth's white-furred gown into a gay, green mantle! Doth it not?"

"Hush, hush!" cried Goodwife Partridge in affright.

"Take the child with his noisy prattle away! Heard I not but now loud sounds of joyous singing and of mirth?" the Magistrate went on. "Me-thinks 'twas not the singing of holy Psalms!"

He bent his head and with his long nose, sniffed hither and yon. "What odor greets my nostril? Smell I not sweet cakes, cakes made from for-bidden sweetening and baked for Yule?"

The people fell back and not a word was said in reply.

"Ah! Ye need not speak. Me ye cannot deceive."

Angrily he pulled open the door of the Dutch oven still resting among the warm ashes on the hearth. "Baking Yule cakes, is that wherewith ye women waste your time? There . . ." but no, the oven was empty. "Ye've given them to your childer . . ." He looked, but he saw not a mouth that chewed, not a jaw that moved.

Only little God-be-thanked whimpered under the stern gaze. Then the babe's hand darted, swift as a bird, to his mouth and something was popped inside.

"There! A Yule cake! The child hath a Yule cake! Open thy jaws! Show me the cake!"

In a flash, God-be-thanked gulped once, then a second time and the cake was gone. Obediently he opened his mouth and there on his fat red tongue, a telltale line of white crumbs did show, which but angered the Magistrate the more.

He turned to the elders.

"Men!" he cried. "Where are the tools? What hast thou done with axe, knife, auger, pit-saw, frow? Why be ye not at work? Know ye not we must build new homes for the newcomers from the *Fearless*?"

"Our tools are gone to be mended this day, good sir," spoke up one of their number.

"Women!" the Magistrate went on. "Why are thy spinning wheels idle? This is a day of work and no cheer."

"We have no flax, good sir," spoke up one of their number. "We cannot spin without flax."

"No tools! No flax!" snorted the Magistrate. He looked round the room and his eyes lighted on the table board, from which the food and trenchers and pewter had been removed. It shone bright and white in the flickering firelight. "There! The shining board! That proveth there hath been Christmas-keeping there! The shining board . . ."

His eye lingered on it and as Mistress Charity watched him, she thought to herself that his face softened a little. Perhaps he, too, remembered Christmas in Old England, though he dared not confess it. Now, now was the time to speak. So Mistress Charity stepped bravely forth and told the Magistrate that it was she who had helped the children—the little children who had never known what Christmas was—to keep it.

" 'Tis the day of the Lord's birth!" she added softly. "He came to lighten men's hearts. In Old England, 'tis a day of joy and cheer. Joy and cheer are needed in this New England even as in the Old."

The Magistrate listened in amazement and as he listened, his frown grew heavier.

"Thou art frank, Mistress, and brave-spoken," he said. "Thou art new to this land, having but so recently stepped ashore from the *Fearless*. As time passes, thou wilt learn that our ways are not Old England's ways. We left them behind us to make a better life for ourselves here. Our law reads: Whosoever shall be found observing any such day as Christmas or the like, either by forbearing of labor, feasting, or in any other way, shall be fined five shillings or be imprisoned. The edict is work or go to the gaol. But we suspend sentence this once, since thou art a newcomer. See ye, however, that it doth not happen again."

He opened the batten door. On the sill he turned. "Gaffer Partridge!" he called. "Remove this frumpery at once. See that this foolishness doth not happen again." He poked his wooden cane in the greens over the door and pulled them roughly down.

"Ay, good sir!" "Rightly, good sir!" "Thank 'ee, good sir!" obediently answered Gaffer Partridge and his neighbors.

The door closed and the Magistrate was gone. The men and women set to work at once pulling down the Christmas greens. While they worked, they looked at each other and smiled. "We kept Christmas once again—and with out childer, too!" There was a light in their eyes which had not been there before.

After they all went away Aunt Charity gathered the children about her and sat down on the settle.

"Was it wrong then, after all?" asked Seaborn.

"Oh, no!" answered Waitstill. "The greens were so beautiful to see!"

"And Silence Pitkin smiled again and again!" added Comfort. "She was happy for the first time in her life."

"And Preserved Rogers played games so lustily!" Waitstill went on. "We never thought he could play at all."

"And Temperance Seward spoke not once of dying!" added Thankful happily. "She asked if she could come back tomorrow."

"And God-be-thanked swallowed the last Yule cake in the nick of time!" said Aunt Charity, with a laugh. "Well, dear-my-loves," she went on, as the tears filled her eyes, "ye've kept Christmas for the time only! Now hearken well—*That which ye have in your hearts can never be taken away!*"

"Christmas! Christmas!" echoed the children. "We've kept Christmas!"

"And ye'll never forget, will ye?" asked Aunt Charity.

"No, sweet Aunt!" answered the children. "Never shall we forget. That which we have in our hearts can never be taken away!"

Outside the House

Outside the house
The wind blows shrill;
The snow drifts high
Over the sill.
The snow drifts high
    Hiding from view
    The neighbor's house—
    His pine trees too.

Inside the house
The fire burns bright,
Making a circle
Of warmth and light.
The fire burns warm
    Sends welcome heat
    To hearts and hands
    And stone-cold feet.

Over the hill
The wind blows cold,
Driving each beast
Into sheltered fold.
The snow bends over
    Each tree to the ground;
    Covers each footprint
    And muffles each sound.

Within the house
The great logs fall,
Throwing dark shadows
Along the wall.
The logs turn red
    And simmer low,
    With fiery sparks
    That come and go.

HOW CHRISTMAS CAME TO
BLUEBERRY CORNERS

A New England Christmas

THE CONGREGATIONALISTS in New England did not celebrate Christmas. So strong was the Puritanical hold upon the early New England settlers, that Christmas was banned officially for nearly three hundred years. In the early days, all who tried to bring it back were fined or jailed. Not until the middle of the nineteenth century, when Episcopal congregations began to be established, did Christmas make a feeble comeback. Its taking over was a gradual process, for many neighborhoods did not do so until after 1900. In the 1940's, in a rural Connecticut town, I talked to men and women who had never celebrated Christmas in their youth, and who still mildly disapproved of it, although they and their families had taken over its outward aspects.

Becky and Fanny were two of the eight children of Parson Griswold, who lived at Blueberry Corners in northwest Connecticut in 1840. There were not many pleasures in their lives, for they wore hand-me-down clothes and the shelves in the Parson's kitchen were often empty. Most of the people in town were Meeting House people; that is, they "went to Meeting" each Sunday and listened to Parson Griswold preach. The Meeting House was never called a church. Only the Episcopalians had churches.

17

A new family came to town, and Becky and Fanny talked to a new girl at school, Julie Ann Janeway, who wore beautiful clothes and went to the *church* at Blueberry Center. They listened with bright eyes and open mouths when Julie Ann told them about something called *Christmas* Becky and Fanny had never heard the word before, and finally . . . Becky felt she had to do something about it.

"Do you have gingerbread *every* day, Julie Ann Janeway?" asked Becky. "With icing on it?"

"Yes," said Julie Ann. "Here, you can have it. I'm sick of gingerbread."

"Don't want it," replied Becky, turning her back and walking on. The two girls were walking slowly home from school. On her head, instead of a shawl, Julie Ann wore a velvet bonnet with a plume on one side. Her long coat, which was called a pelisse, had buttons all the way down the front.

It was mid-December and the snow in the road was packed hard and smooth. The farmers had broken it out with their ox teams in the early morning. The sky had a heavy, gray, sullen look as if another snowstorm were threatening.

"Just wait till Christmas comes!" boasted Julie Ann. "We'll have better things than gingerbread then. We'll have plum pudding and . . ." All the way home, Julie Ann talked of some strange, mysterious thing which she called "Christmas."

"What's that?" asked Becky, drawing in her breath sharply. "What's Christmas?"

"It's the day the Lord Jesus was born!" said Julie Ann, with an important air. "It comes on the twenty-fifth of December and we go to church to see the illumination and we have a tree!"

"But Pa didn't say so!" objected Becky.

"Your pa?" laughed Julie Ann. "Why should he say so?"

"Guess he's the Parson o' the Ecclesiastical Society o' Blueberry Corners! Guess he knows 'bout everything!" Becky drew her breath again in sharp defiance. "But he didn't say nothin' 'bout Christmas."

"Oh, we don't go to the Meeting House!" replied Julie Ann. "I meant at the Episcopal Church at Blueberry Center; that's where we go. Oh, I just love Christmas, don't you?"

"I never saw one—what are they like?" asked Becky, her curiosity getting the better of her. She might well have added that she had never heard of one, but she did not.

"Oh, Becky Griswold!" cried Julie Ann, clapping her hands in rapture. "They're the most elegantest things you ever saw!"

"What are?" asked Becky. "You haven't told me what you are talking about yet."

"Oh, the tree and the candles and the Yule log and the presents . . ."

"How do you do it?" asked Becky soberly. Fanny and the other children crowded round to listen, their eyes open wide with expectation.

"Well," said Julie Ann, "we find the most beautiful spruce tree in the woods and we hang it all over with gold and silver apples. For buds and flowers, all over the branches, we hang sugar almonds, sugarplums,

gilded walnuts, cinnamons, gum balls and all kinds of sweetmeats. And all over the tree there will be a thousand little candles to shine among the dark branches, and around the bottom all kinds of beautiful presents . . ."

"Presents? What are they?" asked Becky. The children crowded closer.

"Why, *presents*!" cried Julie Ann. "Haven't you ever had any presents, Becky? Never in your life?"

"No," said Becky, slowly. "What are they?"

"Things people give to you," replied Julie Ann.

"Oh, yes, Becky!" cried Fanny, eagerly. "Don't you remember? Mr. Butterfield, the peddler, gave us each a string of beads."

"Yes," said Becky, "and I had another present, too. Aunt Leteshy gave me her old red flannel petticoat when it got worn out, and Ma made a Meetin'gown out of it."

"A red flannel petticoat!" sniffed Julie Ann. "I wouldn't want a worn-out petticoat, I'm sure. I mean lovely things. Oh, just everything you can think of, Becky Griswold."

"What? Tell us," begged the children, their eyes opening wider.

"Well," said Julie Ann, "I expect I shall have a pretty doll, the prettiest doll that ever was, all dressed in grown-up clothes. And a silk cloak with quilted lining, and my little brother wants a new stick pony to gallop on. It doesn't matter what it is. Anything can come at Christmas!"

"Oh, I wish somebody'd give me a pretty doll!" cried Becky, impulsively. Then she bit her lips, for well she knew they wouldn't.

Suddenly it seemed dreadful to be the Parson's children. It meant being poorer than anybody else. It meant wearing heavy calfskin shoes instead of morocco buskins like Julie Ann's. It meant homespun gowns instead of muslin delaine or bombazette, and sunbonnets instead of gypsy bonnets. No, there were too many mouths to feed in Parson Girswold's home. As Ma said so often, they ought to be thankful for *small* blessings and surely the blessings were small enough. There would never be any Christmas in the Parson's family. Becky's eyes filled with tears.

"Here, take a bite of my gingerbread, please!" begged Julie Ann. She came close, put her arm in Becky's and with the other hand pressed the gingerbread upon her. Becky gulped down a bite, then tried to say, "Don't want your old gingerbread!" but she couldn't, for her mouth was too full and it tasted good, oh, so good.

"Don't Christmas ever come to Blueberry Corners where you live?" asked Julie Ann, when they came to the parting of the ways.

"Of course Christmas comes to our house!" Becky burst out indignantly.

Why should Julie Ann have everything, satin aprons, gypsy bonnets, gold rings, ruffled pantalets, and Christmas, too? She was filled with sudden rage and jealousy. "Of course we have Christmas!" Then she turned on her heel and ran. She ran a long distance along the road before she stopped. It was as if she were running away from herself, for she knew that what she had said was not true at all, and her heart beat heavily within her. A little later Fanny caught up with her and put her arm around her waist.

"Is it true?" she asked, her blue eyes shining like stars. "Oh, I do so want to have Christmas! If we could only have one Christmas, that would be enough."

"Why, Fanny Griswold!" said Becky, sharply. "Course we can't and you ought to know it. I could shake you for acting so silly. I only said that 'cause . . . I didn't know what else to say. We can't have Christmas. We're too poor. We didn't even have turkey on Thanksgiving. And there's never any money for new clothes. That's why we always wear hand-me-downs. I thought you knew that . . . I thought that's why you went to Happy Valley . . ."

"Oh!" said Fanny, thoughtfully. "If I'd only known about Christmas sooner, I'd have told Great-Aunt Mehitable *that*, too, and she could have come for a visit and brought heaps of Christmas presents . . ."

"You spoiled it all, by tellin' her we needed so many things," scolded Becky. "There's no use thinkin' of her. She don't even come to see us any more like she used to."

It was true and both girls knew it. Great-Aunt Mehitable had not been heard from since Fanny's abrupt departure from Happy Valley. The time of her customary fall visit had passed. She had not come or sent any word. Everybody knew that she was offended and no more help could be expected. Things were worse than before Fanny went. Mrs. Griswold and Aunt Leteshy got cross whenever her name was mentioned. It was best not to speak of her, or even to think of her.

"Oh, dear!" wailed Fanny, unhappily. "I do so want a Christmas—so there!"

"You ought to have more sense, Fanny!" scolded Becky.

But somehow or other, Fanny would never learn sense. She would never be as practical as Becky. She kept on wishing and hoping. At the supper table that night, she broke out again: "I'll be glad when Christmas comes!" Her serene faith lighted up her small thin face.

Becky tried to kick her under the table with her foot, but could not reach far enough. Besides, it was too late. Ma and Aunt Leteshy had both heard and so had the rest of the family, all the brothers and little sisters whose heads and elbows showed above the rim of the long table— Benjamin and David, Polly Prue, Lucinda Jane, Sarah Ann, and even baby Matthew. They all began to stir and clamor and cry, "Oh, what is it?" and "We want it, too!" and "Tell us about it, Fanny, do!"

"Julie Ann Janeway told us about it at school." Fanny's little voice rang out high and clear. "It's coming soon, on the twenty-fifth of this month."

"But it's not coming *here*!" protested Becky. "She never said it was coming here!" She wished Fanny were not so stupid, for she saw by her mother's face that this was a serious matter.

"Nonsense!" said Mrs. Griswold, emphatically. "What's the child thinking of? We're not Episcopal; that's why we don't believe in keeping those prayerbook days, like Christmas and Easter. It's only the Church of England that does that. They have a little church down to Blueberry Center now, I hear. But we don't keep it at the Meeting House and that's the long an' short on't."

"But can't we have 'presents' like Julie Ann Janeway?" wailed Fanny. "We want presents!" chimed in Polly Prue and the little sisters.

"Presents!" snapped Mrs. Griswold. "What be ye thinkin' of? Here we are all a-scrimpin' and a-savin' and a-workin' our heads off just to get clothing to cover you and food to fill you up and wood enough to warm you and you want presents!"

"It's a right nice custom," said Aunt Leteshy quietly. "I wish we could have it!"

"Don't help put more notions in their heads," said Mrs. Griswold sharply. "School keeps that day same as any other. You'll be good children; forget this nonsense and do your duty."

When Parson Griswold returned from making a sick call, Ma asked him to explain. He went to his study, looked through a pile of musty books, and then his face turned sober as he spoke. The children folded their hands and listened. "Nobody knows when Christ was born, and there is nothing in the Bible to tell us when to keep Christmas," he said. "The disciples and early Christians did not keep Christmas, and no mention is made of its recognition until after the fourth century. Then there were some who said it was on the twentieth of May, which is every bit as likely as the twenty-fifth of December."

It sounded just like one of his long sermons in Meeting. Becky and Fanny looked at each other and wondered what all his big words had to do with Julie Ann's tree and presents.

"It was kept for many years in England," Pa went on, "but it became a celebration of boisterous revelry, in which people forgot the true meaning of Christ's birth. So when our ancestors came to found New England two hundred years ago, they gave up celebrating all the saints' days, along with many Old World customs and practices, which they disapproved of. They came to New England to begin all over again, so they could live better and have their children live better. Our Puritan fathers escaped from the yoke of bondage and fought hard for their liberty by prayers, toils, tears, and sacrifice in a new land. It is our duty to walk in the good old ways which they have laid down for us. So, children, do your duty, be obedient, study your catechism, say your prayers, and forget this talk of Christmas."

The row of eyes around the room closed in respectful silence and not a murmur was heard during the reading of the chapter from the Bible and the prayers which followed.

But Becky could not sleep for thinking of Christmas. She had not understood all her father's statements, but she knew that the idea of Christmas, entrancing and enticing as it was, when painted in glowing colors by the words of Julie Ann Janeway, was somehow wrong and forbidden. Others might enjoy it, but not the Parson's family. Becky's heart sank within her. No, they could not have it, except by some miracle. She folded her hands and prayed earnestly.

The days went by slowly, one after the other. Fanny was not sensible at all and her blue eyes shone more and more like stars. Every day Becky scolded her, but she and the little sisters became more and more confident. Julie Ann Janeway began to talk of a red merino coat trimmed with swansdown and other unheard-of things. When she asked daily, "Don't Christmas ever come to Blueberry Corners?" Becky protested vigorously, "Course it does! Guess we can have Christmas, too, if we want." Every night Becky prayed. On the night of the twenty-fourth, over their supper of bread and hasty pudding and applesauce, Becky saw the row of eyes of her brothers and sisters shining with bright expectancy, at the thought of what would happen on the morrow. That night she prayed again for a miracle.

When she awoke on Christmas morning, all her dreams faded away before the sternness of reality. She heard the thumping of clothes in the pounding barrel. It was wash day, not Christmas. Her mother's voice called her at daylight. A heavy snow had fallen the night before. Snow had drifted in through the cracks in the unplastered wall and a great drift lay across the bed. She gathered up the quilt and shook the snow off on the floor, then she put it back on the blankets and tucked Fanny and Polly Prue up snugly. The room was very cold. She shivered as she pulled her clothes on. When she went down the step stairs into the kitchen, nothing was different. No miracle had happened. There were the usual chores to do: breakfast to get, cows to be milked, children's faces to wash, hair to comb, lunches to pack.

"Shall I put on my Meeting gown?" asked Fanny, when she came down, supreme in her faith. "Don't we go to Meeting on Christmas?"

"Land sakes!" cried Mrs. Griswold. "Is the child crazy? Ain't she forgot that Christmas nonsense yet?"

At the usual time the children were packed off to school with their lunches. They waded in the heavy snow up to their knees. The first thing they noticed was that Julie Ann Janeway was absent.

Becky Griswold thought hard all morning. By noon she had worked out a philosophy of her own. She remembered how hard she had to work, spinning shoe-thread for two weeks, to earn her new pair of calfskin shoes. You have to work for it before you get it. Her brothers and her little sisters were waiting and trusting. Becky must make a miracle happen.

At nooning, Becky put her thoughts into action. She left the schoolhouse and started off across a field. Behind her Fanny called frantically and then came running up, her hair flying.

"Where are you going, Becky?" she demanded.

Becky's face was very solemn. "Do you want Christmas to really and truly come?" she asked.

"Oh, yes," cried Fanny, eagerly. "Do you think it will?"

"I'm going to get Christmas for all of us," said Becky. "You must go back and say nothing."

"Oh, Becky, I'm so glad," said Fanny. "I just knew Christmas would come!" Then she ran back to her seat at the schoolroom.

Becky soon left the field and went back to the main road, where walking was easier, for the road had been broken out during the morning. When she reached home, she peeped in at the back door. She had one last hope that Christmas might have arrived during her absence. But, no—Aunt Leteshy and Mrs. Whipple, from the farm next door, and Ma were spinning. The washing was done, but the kitchen was more upset than ever. She put her hands over her ears to shut out the sad, moaning wail of the spinning wheels. The mournful sound gave her a deep discomfort.

She smelled a parsnip stew simmering in the big kettle over the fire. She hated parsnip stew. It always meant there was not enough pork to go round, so they would have to fill up on parsnips. She pressed her hand on her stomach and thought how good a sausage, nicely browned and sizzling, would taste. It had been a long time since she had tasted one.

Becky knew now that she would have to find Christmas herself. Before she reached the woodshed, she had made up her mind what she would do. She found a hatchet and hid it under her coat. How thankful she was that her mother and aunt were busy and had not seen her! Her father, too, buried among the books in his study, rarely noticed what was going on, unless it was brought to his attention. Becky flew down the hill again, but she did not return to school.

She went to the village and on her way she passed Julie Ann Janeway's house—a great, white square mansion with green blinds, which sat snugly behind a white picket fence. She stared at it—then suddenly there was Julie Ann at her side, pulling and tugging, dragging her in. Inside the house, she saw a merry crowd around the table, singing and laughing and eating. In a corner of the next room, she saw the tree covered with lighted candles! She gasped as she looked. It was more beautiful than anything she had ever seen in her life!

Julie Ann wore a yellow silk gown with ruffles and her hair hung over her shoulders in a shower of curls. She jumped and danced about gaily, pointing out her array of gifts. There were the pretty doll and the red merino coat and her little brother's stick pony, just as she had said.

Becky held her arms crossed tightly over her thin chest to keep the hatchet under her coat from slipping. Her coat was too small for her. Her hands were bare and her wrists showed red and raw below her sleeves. Her little head shawl was tied firmly in a knot under her chin. She stood stiffly and stared. Then she shivered and turned away. Julie Ann pressed a large chunk of candied gingerbread upon her, but she did not take it.

"Don't Christmas ever come to Blueberry Corners?" asked Julie Ann, this time sympathetically.

"Course it does!" cried Becky, as she went out the door.

Down the road she flew as fast as her thin legs would carry her. As she passed Mr. Webb's store, she stopped for a moment and pressed her nose against the glass window. She saw a fine array of sugar animals, peppermint sticks, and lozenges, but she did not linger long over the impossible. She went through the burying ground behind the Meeting House, wading in the deep snow over the graves of her ancestors. She stopped and looked up through the black, drooping branches of the great pines. Their snowy boughs hung so low she had to stoop to walk under them. They were beautiful trees, but much too large.

She went on and on, climbing over the big hill beyond. Here she came to a pine grove, with tall sentinel pines reaching far up to touch the sky. There was very little snow among the pine needles and walking was easier. At length she came out in a pasture where many seedling pines and spruces had sprung up. She examined the small trees carefully. One

was too large, one too small, one bent or crooked. Was there one as pretty as Julie Ann's?

At last she found a perfect tree. It was just a little taller than she was herself. Her hands had grown cold and stiff without mittens. She took the hatchet from under her coat, tied the little head shawl tighter under her chin, and began to chop. The trunk of the tree was sturdy and the hatchet was not very sharp. She chopped as hard as she could and her hands became warmer. The trunk was nearly ready to fall, when somehow the hatchet slipped and fell against her shoe.

Becky looked down at her foot and there in the snow which had been white like the wool on a sheep's back, she saw a spot of bright red. She wondered how it came there. It grew larger and larger as she watched. She looked more closely and then she saw that a gash had been cut in her new calfskin shoes—the shoes she had worked so hard to earn and which were to last till next summer. Suddenly she hid her face in her hands and burst into tears; then she crumpled up on the ground.

Some time later, she roused herself and could not seem to remember what had happened. She was very cold and stiff and could scarcely move. The sun was sinking slowly behind the pine-clad hill. It must be late. Then she saw the tree lying on its side and she remembered. She must hurry and bring Christmas to the children or they would all be disappointed. She tried to get up but she couldn't. Her foot hurt badly, but she was determined to reach home somehow. Over the brow of the hill she saw smoke rising from a chimney. It was Old Hiram Curtis's cottage, down in Cedar Hollow, a quarter of a mile away. She began to make her way toward it, crawling inch by inch on her knees.

Becky never knew how she got there, but she did. She made her way over the snowy hill, crawled over several stone walls, under a rail fence and finally came in sight of Old Hiram's woodpile. Fortunately he was there, picking up an armful of wood. He dropped it hastily and came forward limping, for he was crippled, when he heard her feeble voice calling.

"Dew tell, child!" he exclaimed, scratching his head in perplexity. "Wal, ef it ain't Becky Griswold, the Parson's darter, sure 's I'm alive, a-crawlin' on all fours. Whatever ails ye? Oh, goodness gracious, I must call Mirandy, she'll know what to do. Just you wait now."

He limped down the hill as quickly as he could and in a few moments Mirandy came with a wooden sled. The two old people helped Becky on and dragged her to the back door. Then they carried her in to a bed in the corner of the kitchen and Old Mirandy bandaged up her foot and treated her hands and feet for frostbite.

"I'd like to take you home, Becky," said Old Hiram. "Dark's a-comin' on and the Parson'll be worried, I haven't a doubt . . ."

Suddenly Becky remembered the tree and the hatchet which she had left on the hillside. She told Old Hiram and he went at once to fetch them. By the time he returned, it was dark. The mountain road which led to their cottage had not been broken out and as he had only one poor, lame horse, he could not take her home. Becky's foot began to pain her and finally she fell into a fitful sleep.

That afternoon, when the children came home from school and Becky was not with them, Mrs. Griswold questioned Fanny.

"She went to get our Christmas! She went to get our Christmas," said Fanny over and over again, her eyes full of tears.

"Still talking foolishness!" cried Mrs. Griswold. "When will that child learn to be sensible?"

By nightfall, Becky's mother was alarmed and anxious. The younger children were put to bed whimpering. When Parson Griswold returned late in the evening, he too was alarmed. He walked to all the near neighbors to make inquiries, but no one had seen Becky. Several men went to the village to ask about her, but returned without news of any kind. Mrs. Griswold sat up all night, but Becky did not come.

The next morning, Fanny continued to insist, "She went to get our Christmas!" so Parson Griswold stopped in at the Janeway house. There Julie Ann and Mrs. Janeway told him of Becky's visit on the previous day, but the incident threw no light on her present whereabouts. He left to join the other searchers. Word had spread like wildfire through the little community that Becky Griswold was missing. The Meeting House bell was rung and a search party set out at once to scour the woods and hillsides.

After Parson Griswold left the Janeway house, Julie Ann began to cry. "Oh, Mother," she wailed, "it's all my fault. I was so selfish, I bragged about Christmas all the time, and about all the things I was going to get. It's all my fault that she's lost." Mrs. Janeway took her repentant daughter in her arms and listened in silence. "Becky said she never had a tree and never had a present except a string of cheap glass beads and a hand-me-down petticoat in her whole life," Julie went on in distress. "Oh, Mother, let's make Christmas all ready for Becky to see when she comes back! I'm sure they'll find her, aren't you? She wanted Christmas so much, and so did Fanny."

At the parsonage, Mrs. Griswold met many visitors at the door, fresh hope arising with each arrival. "Have you seen her? Have you seen Becky?" she cried over and over. Then, frantic, she fell back again into despair: "Oh, they'll never find her! She's lost on the mountain. She was out in the snow all night. Oh, Becky, my child, my child!" She threw her apron over her head and sobbed.

"Don't, Ma, please!" said Fanny. "She'll come, Ma, I know she will. She's just gone to get us a Christmas!" Fanny was the only sensible one now, the only one who did not cry. Her faith never wavered for an instant. She kept her mother and aunt and all the children quiet, with her faith in Becky's return.

When Mrs. Janeway and Julie Ann appeared at the door, bearing in their arms Julie's beautiful tree and a host of presents, Mrs. Griswold sniffed, "Christmas nonsense! We don't hold to that! That's what caused all the trouble!" but she could not refuse them entrance. The other neighbor women crowded round to see and hear when Julie Ann and her mother explained. They were all Meeting House people and had never heard about Christmas, but the idea appealed to them. Worn and anxious with worry and waiting, it gave them something to do. Then, too, they had seen the empty shelves of their Parson's kitchen and they were ashamed. Quickly the word passed from one to the other; one by one they went home to return again with cakes and gingerbread, hams, sides of bacon, pots of beans, baskets of apples, potatoes, groceries, jugs of cider, blankets, clothing, and an assortment of sweets from Mr. Webb's store.

Christmas Day had passed and on the following afternoon Becky still lay abed in the little Curtis cottage. A deep cold had settled on her chest and all night she had been feverish. Old Aunt Mirandy sat by her bed and held her hand. "There, there, now, don't 'ee move!" she said comfortingly. She got up and brewed a steaming bowl of thoroughwort tea. "Just take a drink o' this, child," she coaxed. "It'll hearten you up consid'ble." Becky sat up and drank dutifully.

"Hiram's gone to git a bobsled and team from Eddie Wheeler," the old woman went on. "Eddie was here this mornin' and told us the hull town's been out a-searchin' for the Parson's darter. Think of that, now! See how they missed you, dearie? We aim to git you home 'fore nightfall and the ride won't hurt you a mite."

A half hour later the bobsled came and with it several men. They placed an old mattress on the sled and Becky was moved onto it carefully and covered with blankets and a bearskin. Old Hiram fastened her pine tree up in front and the sight of its green waving branches gave her comfort. She waved her hand to the old couple by the door as the oxen began to move.

On the way home Becky was surprised to hear bells ringing and to see people walking along beside the sled and behind it. Becky wondered what was the matter. Her chest was so tight, she could not cough or speak aloud and her foot pained badly. As the procession drew up to the parsonage she saw that there were people there, too.

"The Lord be praised!" cried Parson Griswold and his wife, as they rushed out the door.

"Oh, Ma!" said Becky, hoarsely. "I didn't mean to cause you trouble. I only wanted to get a little tree for us—but I guess I ketched a bad cold!"

"There! There, child!" cried Mrs. Griswold. "It's all right. Oh, how thankful we are to get you back again."

Becky was carried indoors by willing hands and put to bed in the north chamber. There she rested a while, happy and content to be at home again, then slept a little.

It was evening when she opened her eyes again. Beside her stood a little green spruce tree without trimming of any kind, plain and unassuming as it grew in the woods. She reached out her hand and touched the needles tenderly. Then she looked up. At the foot of the bed, she saw another tree, laden with gold and silver apples, sugar almonds and gilded walnuts, cinnamons and gum balls. Through its dark branches gleamed the light of many candles. On the table beneath was piled an array of presents—among them a pretty doll and a red merino coat. There were many other things as well, enough for every one of Becky's brothers and sisters. As Becky saw all their heads crowding eagerly about the tree and heard their delighted exclamations, she felt a deep peace in her heart.

Parson Griswold came and sat by her bedside and the children hushed their voices and listened as he read the story of the birth of Christ from the Bible and then prayed from a heart overflowing with gratitude. Becky was surprised to see the faces of neighbors peering round the bed— the Whipples, Aunty Ruth Hodges and Sally, Mr. Webb, Miss Cynthy Hawkes, Dan Russell, and others. She was surprised to see most of the women wipe tears from their eyes. Aunt Leteshy smiled happily.

Then Julie Ann Janeway came to her bedside and put the lovely doll in her arms and murmured something about being sorry.

"Oh, is it for me?" asked Becky. "I never thought I would have one for myself!"

"Yes, it's for you, to keep for always!" said Julie Ann, with a radiant smile. Then she turned and slipped away.

Becky could not understand what had happened. It was all very strange and too good to be true. It must be a miracle! The miracle she had prayed for so hard.

"Did Christmas come after all?" she asked.

"Yes, child," said her father, "because you brought it. You have shown us the true spirit of Christmas, by thinking of others more than yourself. From this time on, we shall have Christmas every year, for we truly need it."

"So Christmas came to Blueberry Corners after all!" said Becky softly.

"I knew it would!" said Fanny, and her eyes shone like stars.

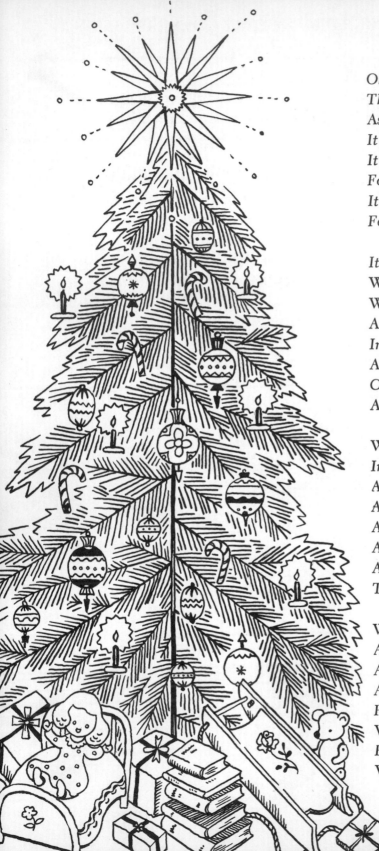

Tree with Lights

Oh, see
The great big Christmas tree,
As gay as can be!
It shines so bright,
It lights the dark night
For me.
It lights up the world
For all to see.

It shines and twinkles
With silver and gold,
With bells and stars
And garlands rolled
In and out
And roundabout,
Circling around
And touching the ground.

With lights that sparkle
In colors gay,
And tinsel that twinkles
And drips away;
And balls that glitter
And whirl and shine,
And garlands that round
The branches twine.

With toys and books and lollipops
And candy canes and wooden tops,
And skates and sleds
And dolls and beds
For all the children
Who love it well;
For young and old
Who love to tell
    The story of Christmas.

THE PINK CHINA BONBON DISH

A Small-Town Ohio Christmas

CHRISTMAS has always been a period of deep joy and gladness to all Lutherans. It was Martin Luther who first used the evergreen tree as its symbol, and *O Tannenbaum* has always been a favorite German Christmas song. Many other German customs, including the baking of *sprengerli* and *pfeffernuesse*, were common in west central Ohio in the early 1900's. This was before the days of the automobile, when life was simpler, centered around a smaller area governed largely by the family horse-and-buggy. Perhaps one reason why Christmas assumed such vast importance in family life at that time, was the lack of other competition in the way of celebration or diversion. Children moved in small circles, met fewer people, traveled little, and made most of their own amusements out of their own creativity and ingenuity. Premanufactured entertainment was never handed out to them.

The Pink China Bonbon Dish is a fictionized account of my own Ohio childhood Christmas. The characters are myself, Lottie, my brothers and sisters and my parents, my father being the minister of the local Lutheran Church. Other characters are based on actual people I knew and remember well to this day. Our Christmas was never distinctly German, however, for my mother was not German and never took on the local German customs.

In 1939, my sister Miriam wrote me of our childhood:

"Christmas was just about the grandest thing that could ever happen. I will always remember it as the bright light of the year.

35

One of the nice things about it was that it lasted! It was so long in coming and made anticipation so great. Other things got over so quickly but not Christmas at Anna! Weeks before, we made plans and started thinking about presents to make. We spent days and weeks in hiding, making pillow-tops, aprons, pen-wipers, calendars, covering boxes with cretonne, etc.

"One Christmas I saw a dish in a downtown store which I wanted to get for Mama. I looked at it daily for weeks. It was a divided dish, with a handle—and it was very expensive. I suppose now that Mama had no earthly use for it, but I wanted her to have it . . . How I ever managed to pay for it . . ."

This was the spark for my story. Miriam did not actually have as great difficulties in acquiring the pink china bonbon dish as Mina did, but the entire story gives the authentic flavor of the Ohio Christmases of my childhood. My brothers and sisters will see themselves again as children. Books were always the most valued of the gifts we received; and giving presents of our own making to both Mama and Papa was equally important. The church members' share in their minister's Christmas was also typical. How wonderful were those simple Christmases of my childhood!

"Oh, Lottie," cried Mina, "Elsie Prince is going to get a red silk dress for Christmas!"

"How do you know?" asked Lottie, looking at her sister sharply. In her hands she held a pillow-top of huck-toweling and round her neck hung strands of black and orange embroidery floss. As she spoke she wove her needle in and out of the linen, drawing the floss through in intricate design.

The two little girls, aged eight and ten, sat on the edge of their bed in the upstairs bedroom. The room was unheated, save for a "drum" which was in reality an enlarged stovepipe from the stove in the room below and which gave off no noticeable heat.

"She saw her mother sewing on it last night," answered Mina. "She got up out of bed and went downstairs to get a drink of water. The door was open a crack and she peeped in."

"She did?" cried Lottie. The look of surprise on her face changed suddenly to soberness. She shook her head. "Well, Elsie's Christmas is spoiled now," she said. "I wouldn't want to know beforehand what I was going to get. I'd rather have a surprise on Christmas."

"Yes, so would I," added Mina thoughtfully. "But a red silk dress *would* be nice, wouldn't it?"

"There are many things better than red silk dresses," said sensible Lottie. "Have you decided yet what you are going to give to Mama?"

"Oh, yes!" exclaimed Mina, "I've been thinking of lots of things—a new coffee pot or a new dressing sack and apron or a lovely pink china bonbon dish . . ."

"There's some blue-checked gingham in that roll of scraps that Aunt

Wilhelmina sent us," interrupted Lottie, practically. "It will be just enough for an apron for Mama—sort of small kitchen apron to be worn on top of her big ones. Mama will like it every bit as much as my pillow-top, if you sew it by hand."

"But I don't like to sew!" protested Mina.

"Why not?" asked Lottie.

"The needle is too fat and it always comes unthreaded," answered Mina dolefully. "The thread gets into knots and I can't make little stitches."

"But you could try hard this time and sew better," counseled Lottie. "Surely, if you love Mama . . ."

"It's too cold up here to sew," wailed Mina. "My fingers are like ice. I couldn't even hold a needle."

"If we did it downstairs, Mama would see us, and it would spoil her surprise," replied Lottie.

"I'd rather give her a bonbon dish," said Mina, stubbornly setting her jaw. "I saw such a pretty one in the window of Mr. Werdenhoff's store."

"But you have no money," protested Lottie. "You can't buy fancy things like bonbon dishes. *Besides*, Mama is too sensible. She doesn't like fancy things."

Mina had to admit that her sister was right. She watched Lottie cut the blue-checked gingham into lengths and heard her explain how it should be put together.

That afternoon Mina was sent to Werdenhoff's store for a gallon of coal oil. Dressed in her knitted hood and warm coat and overshoes, she scurried along in the snow, swinging the coal-oil can at her side. When she reached the store she did not go in at once. She pressed her nose against the glass and looked at the lovely bonbon dish. Surrounded by a miscellany of objects—shoes, bolts of yard goods, jar rubbers, and tin-ware—stood the precious piece of china. It was like none other in the world, for it was in two separate divisions, with a handle between and its delicate pink surface was sprinkled over with flowers. Little Mina wondered what bonbons were. It was Elsie Prince who had told her what the dish was for. Elsie had said it was elegant to have a bonbon dish and Mina decided then and there that nothing was too good for Mama.

Mina knew she must be practical. Bonbon dishes, like other things in stores, cost money. As she pressed her nose against the glass, she began to think of ways of earning money. Once she had picked almost a quart of wild strawberries along the railroad track and Grandma Nagelberger had paid her ten cents for them. But it was winter now and there were no strawberries to be picked. She thought of hoeing the potato patch for Frederick—*he* had money, because he carried the *Cincinnati Times-Star* to most houses in town and he could afford to pay her a nickel for doing his hoeing. But there were no potatoes to be hoed at this time of year. She might piece a quilt, like Lottie's *Irish Chain* or *Fruit Basket*, and sell it at the fair. Quilts were worth several dollars and would buy ever so many bonbon dishes. But no one who sewed as badly as Mina could make a quilt, even if she tried to her dying day. She thought of Lizzie, her grown-up sister, and how she had earned four dollars getting subscriptions to the *Woman's Home Companion* from all the women in Papa's congregation. But all these ways of earning were closed to little Mina.

Suddenly the door of the store opened and a man came out. It was Mr. Werdenhoff himself. "You want something?" he asked gruffly. "Time to close up store and go home to supper."

Mina stumbled over the coal-oil can at her feet and that reminded her. Inside the store it was nearly dark, for no lamps had been lit. She had been looking at the bonbon dish longer than she realized. The lamps at home needed filling. She took the filled can from the storekeeper's hand, replaced the small potato on the end of the spout, to keep the oil from spilling, called "Charge it, please!" and left the store.

Every day Christmas came a day nearer. On Saturday, a week before, Papa and Mama Peterson decided to drive to Simmons. They didn't say why they were going, but all the children knew it had to do with Christmas and avoided acting curious, knowing that that was what was expected of them.

The last thing Mama said before she went out the door was, "Lottie, be sure to stir the mincemeat on the back of the stove. Lizzie, wash up the kitchen floor and take the bread out of the oven as soon as it is nicely browned. Don't do any reading until your work is done. Richard, practice for half an hour, and Frederick, be sure to look after the fires."

"You girls have it easy," grumbled Lizzie, after the sleigh had disappeared down the road and the sound of the jingling bells had died away. Lizzie was fifteen and wore her hair in a pompadour. She went to the kitchen, put on an apron, filled her bucket with warm water from the reservoir at one side of the range, and hunted up the scrubbing brush and rag. Lottie followed and stirred the mincemeat which was simmering in a large dish-pan on the stove.

"Well, you're older," replied Lottie. "If I were allowed to put my hair up and my skirts down, the way you do, I wouldn't mind scrubbing the kitchen floor."

"Ugh!" grunted Lizzie, bending to her knees. "I wish I knew how that story in the *Youth's Companion* comes out."

Lottie returned to the sitting room, brought out her pillow-top and Mina's blue-checked apron. Soon both little girls were seated on the sofa, working hard.

After a while, Frederick came in and shook down the ashes of the base burner. Then he opened the top and dumped in a bucketful of coal. After he went out, the girls were left alone again. There were no sounds except the swish-swish of water over the linoleum floor in the kitchen and an occasional grumble or sigh from Lizzie.

Soon the outer door swung open and Richard came in to practice on his violin. Lottie and Mina put their hands over their ears the moment he started. They begged him to go into the parlor and close the sliding door so they could not hear.

"Do you want me to freeze to death?"

"Go into the bedroom, then," cried Lottie.

"It's cold in there, too," answered Richard.

His screeching began again. The girls looked at each other and gritted their teeth. Then an additional noise began. They couldn't tell which direction it was coming from, but they knew that such horrible howling could come only from the throat of a dog—their own old Ponto.

Down fell the sewing and down fell the violin, as the girls, and Richard began a wild search for the howling dog.

"Tie him up in the woodshed!"

"Catch him first," muttered Richard. "Then muzzle him."

He dragged a shaggy black dog from under the sofa. The next moment he snatched from Mina's hands a half-made blue-checked apron and tied it round the dog's mouth and neck. A wild scuffle ensued—dog, girls, boy, embroidery, sewing, chairs, rugs, all mixed up. The apron came untied as the dog ran. Richard pulled it off, then dropped it casually into the bucket of scrubbing water as he chased Ponto through the kitchen. Seated comfortably on the wet floor, Lizzie looked calmly up from her *Youth's Companion*, but scarcely noticed the commotion, so absorbed was she in her story.

When Papa and Mama came home at dusk, they unloaded mysterious packages from the sleigh and disappeared with them into the downstairs bedroom. It was rather hard to explain the boiled-over mincemeat, the burnt bread, and the half-scrubbed floor, but fortunately Mama had her mind on other things, so didn't say much.

It was Lottie who wrung the blue-checked apron out of the scrubbing water and lamented over it.

Mina did not seem to mind her loss a bit. At last her mind was made up. A bonbon dish it must be, and two days before Christmas she stopped at the store to get it. There were a good many people in Mr. Werdenhoff's store when Mina went in. She had to stay until they were all waited on, for she knew that Mr. Werdenhoff never paid attention to children when he had grown-up customers.

While she was waiting, Mina watched Miss Greta Klopp in the next room, which was her millinery store. A wide, open door divided the two adjoining rooms, so that people could buy hats and groceries and chicken feed all at the same time. Miss Klopp was a tall woman who had an annoying habit of lifting her head and looking down the sides of her nose at you. She reminded Mina of a horse about to neigh.

Miss Klopp was arranging her hats. Many of them were very beautiful, with plumes, feathers, and ribbons. Lottie and Mina admired them so much that they had a hard time to decide which ones they liked best. Miss Klopp put one on a stand in her show-window and then another. Then she would take them out and put others in, go out on the sidewalk and squint her eyes to see how they looked, then come back and do it all over again. After that she spent a long time dusting the tables off and polishing the mirrors. She stared hard in Mina's direction once, so the little girl turned back to the potatoes and horse collars again.

At last all the customers except Mina had left the store. She approached the storekeeper shyly. Mr. Werdenhoff had a bristly mustache and sideburns. His whiskers seemed to spread out in all directions and his black eyes peeped out from under shaggy eyebrows.

He said, "Hey!" so loud, it made Mina jump. "What you want?"

"I want . . . I want . . . the pretty china bonbon dish right there in the window but I haven't any money so I thought I'd make a bargain with you because my Aunt Wilhelmina who lives in Simmons is probably going to give me yard goods for a new dress she usually does on Christmas and I will pay for it with that for it will be worth lots of money." The words came tumbling out as fast as her tongue could say them and her face became pinker and pinker as her eyes sought the floor.

"You want something?" asked Mr. Werdenhoff.

Then Mina remembered how deaf he was. "The pink dish!" she shouted, pointing toward the open shelf.

"Two dollars!" snapped the storekeeper. "Where's your money?"

"But I haven't any . . ." explained Mina.

"No money?" asked Mr. Werdenhoff.

"No," replied Mina. "I thought . . . I thought I would just charge it!"

"Charge it? No, sir, not even if you are the preacher's daughter! Two dollars *cash* is the price! Preachers can't afford such fancy dishes, or if they do, they're getting too much salary!"

His words were cruel and threw Mina into deep despair. She started toward the door, hopeless. She glanced up once and noticed there was no one in sight in the millinery store. In that instant she made up her mind. She stopped for a second beside the show-window, leaned over and picked up the pink china bonbon dish.

She hurried out through the door, with the dish in her arms. As the door closed behind her, a shrill voice from the millinery store called out, "Here! Here! Mina Peterson! Come right back here!"

But Mina flew on feet that were like wings. She never once looked back. As she ran down the back alley in the direction of home, she was filled with happiness, for now, at last, she knew that Mama would have a present—the most beautiful one in the world.

The day before Christmas came. The house was cleaned and scrubbed and dusted. The kitchen was full of freshly baked fruitcakes, mince pies, cookies, and rolls. Then bath time came, with a clothes boiler full of water heating on the kitchen range, besides what was in the reservoir. Mina and Lottie undressed together and Mama washed Lottie first in the tin tub set in the middle of the floor. While Lottie was dressing, Mina had her turn.

"Don't you feel well, Mina?" asked Mama. "You don't seem to have much to say."

"I feel all right," said Mina in a low voice.

Lottie looked at her and thought she looked strange. She decided it was because Mina had no present for Mama. Even when Mina insisted that she did have one, Lottie knew that she was only pretending, as she did so often. She thought of the apron-turned-scrubbing-rag and was very sorry for her little sister.

In the middle of Mina's bath, Mama was called into the sitting room by Lizzie, who said visitors had come.

"Who?" demanded Mina.

"I don't know," replied Lottie, rubbing the towel hard over Mina's back. "I hear a woman's voice . . ."

"Do you think it's . . ."

"Probably Mrs. Weaver with our three pounds of butter for next week or maybe Lena Schweppe and her ma with the turkey. Or it might be Conrad Ludwig and his wife with a basketful of fresh pork for the preacher—they butchered last week."

"Oh!" cried Mina, relieved. "I thought it might be somebody else."

"Are you expecting someone?" asked Lottie.

"No . . . oh, no . . . but I hear footsteps! Somebody's coming down the alley to the woodshed. Are you sure the shades are pulled?"

"Yes, of course," said Lottie. "What makes you so nervous? There, now, you can do your legs yourself." She threw the towel toward her.

"Oh, but it is somebody and they're coming in!" cried Mina. "I can hear them. I don't want them to see me in my skin!"

"The door's locked!" said Lottie stubbornly. Then she stared at Mina and they both listened. The steps came nearer and nearer. Then, suddenly, the back door leading from the woodshed popped open and a man's whiskery head was poked in. "I brought . . ." he began, but his voice died away as he stared.

"Keep out!" "Keep out!" screamed the two girls.

After one hasty look, the intruder banged the door and disappeared.

"Oh! It was Mr. Werden . . . hoff! Mr. Werden . . . hoff!" cried Mina, bursting into tears. "He came to get me, he came to get me! I hate him, I hate him!"

Lottie, who now had her long underwear, ruffled drawers, red flannel and white cotton petticoats on, dashed to the back door and looked round the woodshed, to see if the man had gone. On top of the corncob bin, she saw a large spruce tree, lying on its side.

"It was only Grandpa Nagelberger," she cried, returning. "He's brought our Christmas tree! His bobsled's out front in the road. He's brought our Christmas tree . . . but aren't you glad?"

Mina's eyes were still wet and she looked anything but happy. "He

... shouldn't ... open doors ... without knocking," she gulped.

On Christmas Eve there was the Children's Service at the church, so the girls put on their Sunday clothes after their baths. While at supper, visitors walked in unannounced. Before Mina could run to hide, in came Miss Greta Klopp, milliner, organist, and Sunday-school teacher, followed by Mr. Herman Werdenhoff, storekeeper and Sunday-school superintendent. They both stared at the various members of the family seated round the table and then their eyes rested on Mina at the far end. She trembled from head to foot and somehow made her way to her mother's side and crept up on her lap. That was the only safe place. Above the rumble of her disturbed thoughts she heard them talking to Papa Peterson about choir anthems and hymn singing and the arrangement of the program for that evening.

Suddenly Miss Klopp turned to Mina and said, "Can you speak your piece without forgetting half of it, Mina?"

Mina burst into tears and Mama held her tight in her arms.

"She always learns her piece perfectly, Miss Klopp," answered Mama Peterson quietly.

"I hope she will say it loud!" added Miss Klopp, with relish. "I've noticed that some children shout and yell loud enough on the streets, but in church they cannot speak above a whisper." She gave her head a haughty tilt and stalked out the door. Mr. Werdenhoff followed.

It was after they left that Mina said she did not want to go to the Children's Service. She complained of a pain in her stomach and she looked so pale that everyone believed her. Mama said she was sorry, because she liked to hear her children speak pieces and be proud of them, but all coaxing and argument was of no use. Mama helped Mina take her Sunday clothes off, gave her a dose of medicine, and put her to bed with the hot-water bottle. Lottie kissed her good-bye and promised to tell her all about it afterwards. Lottie felt very lonely to go without her little sister.

When she came home, Mina's eyes shone bright in the lamplight and she said she wasn't sleepy a bit, but she wished Christmas would hurry up and be over. She took the orange and book and box of hard candy which her teacher had sent by Lottie, but did not seem to be interested in Lottie's report. After the light was blown out, she did not talk to Lottie as usual, but tossed and turned a good deal. After a while, queer bumping noises were heard downstairs and the little girls knew that Papa and Mama were downstairs in the parlor trimming the tree that Grandpa Nagelberger had brought. The wind began to howl dismally around the house, and the room turned cold. The two little girls, clad in long woven underwear and outing-flannel nightgowns, curled up in their blankets and soon fell asleep.

Early the next morning they were awakened by a call from Richard: "Get up, it's Christmas!"

"Are you all right, Mina?" asked Lottie, with genuine concern. "It's Christmas and I don't want you to be sick on Christmas."

"I'm all right," whispered Mina, sleepily.

The girls crawled out from under the covers and, feeling their way through the darkness, picked up their clothes. Out in the hall Richard and Frederick were waiting.

"Is Lizzie awake?" asked Lottie.

"No, she wants to sleep," replied Richard. "She's too grown-up for us."

Down the steep, winding stairs the four figures crept quietly. But they did not get far, for a hasty step brought out a loud squeak. In a moment, the stern voice of Papa Peterson come thundering from the downstairs bedroom: "Go back to bed and go to sleep. It's only three o'clock."

Unwillingly, the children returned to their beds and waited what seemed to them an endless length of time. They they started down again only to be halted again by Papa's stern call. Then Mama's voice joined in and Papa said at last, "Very well, then, but be very quiet." The children needed no second invitation. They hurried into the sitting room, which was lighted only by the dull glow through the isinglass panes of the base burner. Frederick lighted a lamp and they waited.

Pretty soon Mama came in, fully dressed, and said she had built the fire in the kitchen stove already. Then Papa called Lizzie from the bottom of the stairs and she came in, blinking sleepily at them. Papa opened the sliding door and took the lamp into the parlor. In a few moments all the candles were lighted on the gaily decorated tree and everyone admired it and said it was the most beautiful tree the Petersons had ever had. Then Papa gave the pitch and the family stood in a row and sang *Silent Night* and *Oh, Come, All Ye Faithful* and other favorite carols. As they sang their eyes were fixed on the little manger scene blow the tree, which looked so living and real in the mysterious candlelight, although all the children knew that Mary and Joseph and the baby Jesus were china dolls and the lake was nothing but a mirror and the woolly lambs would fall over if you touched them. But on this night, these simple things were touched with a heavenly glory which was felt deep in the hearts of all who looked.

After the tree ceremony was over, the children were allowed to look at their gifts and the excitement began. Flying toward the chairs, on which lay the piled-up gifts, the children ran about, crying, "Mine! Mine! Oh, this is for me!" A pile of books for each, hair ribbons and stockings for the girls, knitted mufflers and ready-tied ties for the boys. A sled and a croquet set under the tree. A pair of leggings and a doll's cradle for Mina, a sewing basket and a doll's trunk for Lottie and their old dolls, Beauty and Priscilla, brought back to renewed youth and beauty by means of new heads and complete outfits of new clothes.

Papa and Mama sat around and watched the fun and there were presents for them, too. Calendars and pen-wipers and bedroom slippers and a new student-lamp for Papa. A green jardiniere for Mama from Frederick, bought with his earnings, and a sunflower of cardboard, with pins stuck round the edge for rays, made by Richard at school. Lottie brought forth her black and orange pillow-top and Mama admired the handiwork and said it was just what she needed for the parlor sofa. Frederick and Lizzie tugged and hauled, bringing from the hall closet a large wooden box on castors, with a hinged cover. Upon examination, it was found to be covered on the outside with padded cretonne and lined on the inside with unbleached muslin. When Mama heard that it was intended for her shirtwaists, she smiled and nodded approval and gave both a kiss.

Then it was Mina's turn. She carried her treasured gift carefully and laid it in Mama's lap.

"But what is it, dear?" asked Mama.

"It's . . . it's . . . a bonbon dish . . . at least that's what Elsie Prince said it was . . ." stammered Mina.

"Ha, ha, ha!" laughed the boys. "A bonbon dish!"

"Hush, boys!" said Mama. "Do not laugh at Mina." She began to exclaim over the flowers and the handle and the two handy compartments, but it was easy to see that she was puzzled. She gave Mina a kiss and thanked her; but all the while she kept looking first at the dish and then at her little girl. The rest of the family stared, too, and the boys had a hard time to keep from giggling. What an unusual present for a little girl to give!

Then suddenly Richard spoke his thoughts aloud: "But how could you buy a fancy bonbon dish, Mina, without any money?"

Lottie added, "I thought you didn't have any present for Mama after the apron got torn up!"

Mina answered her promptly: "I had to have something to give to Mama, didn't I? Don't you think, Mama, it's the prettiest bonbon dish in the whole world?"

"It is very pretty, dear," said Mama, still puzzled.

"Where did you get the money?" demanded Richard.

Mina's former anxiety, forgotten for a time in her pleasure over the Christmas gifts, now returned and engulfed her. She trembled, blushed, and looked at the floor. All eyes were turned toward her.

"Did you borrow the money, Mina?" asked Lizzie, looking up from the book she was reading.

"Did you steal it out of somebody's bank?" asked Frederick.

"Children!" called Mama. "Not on Christmas!"

"Oh, I know!" cried Lottie, putting her arms sympathetically about her little sister's shoulder. "You charged it, didn't you, Mina, at Mr. Werdenhoff's store, just as you do the coffee and the coal oil and the other things for Mama?"

But even this explanation did not sound just right, so Papa took things in hand. He drew Mina to his knees and looked hard at her. Mina trembled as she saw the stern look on his face. "How did you come by the dish, Mina?" he asked.

Mina knew she must answer the question. "I . . . I . . . borrowed it from Mr. Werdenhoff's store . . . I mean . . . to pay for it later . . ."

"How do you mean to pay for it?" demanded Papa.

Visions of picking strawberries and hoeing potatoes and getting magazine subscriptions faded away before the sternness of Papa's words. The practical plan which she had suggested to the storekeeper of trading in dress goods sent by Aunt Wilhelmina had not materialized, for Aunt Wilhelmina had sent a croquet set for all five children instead of new dresses. How could she ever pay for the bonbon dish? Mina's heart sank and she could find no words to say. One by one tears rolled down her cheeks.

Through the confusion which followed she heard only a few of Papa's words. Mama's gift was a dishonest one and must be returned the next day.

It was a sad Christmas for little Mina. She watched Richard lacing up Lizzie's high shoes, while Lizzie read aloud to him from his new *Robinson Crusoe*. At breakfast, she barely tasted Mama's delicious twisted rolls covered with white icing or Conrad Ludwig's fresh fried sausage. Even the fifteen-pound turkey brought by Lena Schweppe and her ma, which was too large for the largest platter, was disappointing. And she couldn't beg off going to church, for everyone knew now that she had had no stomachache—only a guilty conscience.

At last Christmas was over, as she had wished it to be. But that did not bring relief, for the hardest part was still to come. Slowly she put on her coat, hood, and mittens and slowly she made her way down the street to Mr. Werdenhoff's store, with the beautiful bonbon dish under her arm. It was as beautiful as ever and her heart ached that Mama could not have it to set on the sideboard.

She opened the door reluctantly. A glance toward the millinery store showed her that Miss Klopp was again rearranging her hats and dusting her fixtures. Mina's heart began to pound, but she did not falter. She knew the meaning of duty and walked along its straight and narrow path obediently.

"I brought it back, Mr. Werdenhoff," she said, setting the dish on the counter.

"Hey? What you want?" cried the storekeeper, holding his hand behind his ear. "You want something?"

Mina pointed to the bonbon dish. "I brought it back!" she shouted, pointing, but Mr. Werdenhoff looked at her as blankly as ever.

"Preachers shouldn't buy such fancy things," he muttered, shaking his head.

Then Mina heard footsteps behind her and without looking, she knew that Miss Greta Klopp stood behind her. It took a great deal of courage to face Miss Klopp and tell her everything, but Mina did so.

"But didn't you know?" cried Mina, after it was all explained. "You called to me to bring it back."

"What?" asked Miss Klopp, in astonishment.

"You saw me take it and you told Mr. Werdenhoff, didn't you?"

"No, I didn't know you had taken anything. I called to you to send a message to Preacher Peterson about the choir anthems, but you were already halfway down the street and didn't hear."

"And you didn't tell Mr. Werdenhoff?" asked Mina, incredulous. "How could I when I did not know?"

Suddenly Miss Klopp began to laugh. She tossed her head back, like a horse neighing, and laughed and laughed. And all the while, her sharp eyes kept staring down the sides of her long nose at poor little Mina. Then she took Mr. Werdenhoff by the arm and explained it all to him in her shrill voice. Mr. Werdenhoff looked extremely puzzled at first and said, "Has the dish been gone? I never even missed it." Then he and Miss Klopp laughed again.

But it wasn't funny to Mina at all. She knew what she must say, and when they stopped laughing, she said it bravely: "I'm sorry I took the bonbon dish because that was stealing. But I still want Mama to have it, so I'll buy it some day *after* I have earned the money . . ." Then she burst into tears.

She never knew how it happened, but suddenly she felt Miss Klopp's arms about her and then she was sitting on Miss Klopp's lap. Mr. Werdenhoff pushed a stick of peppermint candy into one of her hands and the pink china bonbon dish into the other. And Miss Klopp nodded vigorously and told Mr. Werdenhoff that she would go along home with Mina to explain things to Preacher Peterson and his wife herself.

"But," cried Mina, "I can't pay for it until I earn the money. Papa said so."

"There is nothing to pay," said Mr. Werdenhoff gruffly.

"It's a Christmas present for you from Miss Klopp and Mr. Werdenhoff." added Miss Klopp, and a smile spread over her plain face.

"Oh, how can I ever thank you?" cried Mina, happily. "You see, I wanted it so much . . . not for me . . . but for Mama . . ."

Miss Klopp was not terrifying after all and Mr. Werdenhoff was kind and friendly underneath his whiskers. She had misjudged them all along. They were good friends now. She looked down at the pink china bonbon dish in her arms and said tenderly, "Even if Mama hasn't any bonbons, it is still beautiful."

As she went out the door with Miss Klopp, she looked back at Mr. Werdenhoff. His face was one broad smile as he raised his arm to wave good-bye and called, "Merry Christmas, little Mina!"

REGIONAL CHRISTMASES
1940-1967

The Extra Plate

Set the table,
Do not be late;
Be sure to put on
An extra plate.
An extra plate
For the stranger new,
The unknown guest
Passing through.

How little we have
We do not care;
But that little is ours
And we'll always share.
The unknown guest—
Who will it be?
Who will pass by—
We must wait and see.

A sailor, a tramp?
A thief or a cheat?
Yes, with us
He may sit and eat.
A poor old woman,
A rich young queen,
A ghost to scare—
Or a great big bear!

Yes, no matter who,
No matter where;
Anyone is welcome
Whoever he be—
Our portion we share
        Thankfully.

THE UNINVITED GUEST
A Sharecropper Christmas

ALL SUMMER long, the sun rose at four in the morning, as bright as day. In the fall, it shone hot and hard on the backs of men, women, and children, pulling long white sacks behind them through the cotton fields. They followed long rows of cotton, stretching away to the horizon, picking the fluffy bolls and filling their sacks. Picking cotton was a family affair for the sharecropper. Every pound, picked even by a small child, was needed to increase the total. A good crop meant food and clothing for the family for the coming winter, and the chance to stay in their meager cabin for another year.

White cotton seldom brought the cotton family a white Christmas and more often, no Christmas at all. The little snow that fell in Arkansas melted quickly and left a sea of mud. Sometimes someone stepped in, saw their great need, and helped make Christmas for them. It might be a kind neighbor, like J. T. Burgess, who collected the money, penny by penny and dollar bill by dollar bill, to pay the hospital bill after Ricky broke his leg. It might be the boss-man's wife, doing her duty and salving her conscience, bringing the Hutley family an unwanted goose for Christmas.

There were five Hutley children, Mavis and Steve, the older ones, besides Joanda, Ricky, and Lolly, the two-year-old baby. There was Mama and Daddy, too, and the noisy little dog called Trouble. Daddy was a sharecropper, sharing his crop with Charley Shands, the boss-man. He hoped some day to get ahead and have his own team and tools, so he could be a tenant and not have to move every year.

It was because Ricky loved tractors so much that the accident happened. The boss-man's tractor ran over his leg and broke it. That was bad enough, but Mrs. Shands, the boss-man's wife, only made it worse by saying: "I told Dave not to let his kids play around the barn!"

It had happened two weeks before. Now Ricky was back from the hospital with a big cast on his leg. Everybody was happy that he was getting better, even if the kitchen cupboard was almost empty. The days were getting darker and shorter and the cotton was about all picked. There would be several more bales, but the boss-man would get most of it.

Nobody had thought much about Christmas, because there was no money to spend. None of the Hutleys had given a thought to Christmas until Mrs. Shands brought the goose—and said it was for their dinner. It was the goose that changed things.

Mama had to cook it, even if it was tough. She kept it simmering and simmering for hours and hours. The goose gave Mama the idea of getting out her best linen tablecloth, the one she had when she was first married, and that gave big sister Mavis the idea of cutting a little cypress tree down by the bayou . . . Joanda thought of making shiny ornaments out of empty tin cans and Daddy popped popcorn to string. It was fun making Christmas out of nothing!

When Mama called, and the family sat down to eat, they saw that she had lengthened the table and put on an extra plate.

"Who's coming, Mama?" the children asked. "Who's the extra plate for?"

"The uninvited guest!" said Mama.

Mama had been reminded of an old tradition of her Tennessee childhood.

"See, I can walk!"

Ricky raised himself off the bed, walked across it, then slumped awkwardly down again. Trouble jumped up and barked.

"Great stuff!" said Daddy. "We got to git that harness off o' you purty soon."

"You're a turtle in a shell," said Steve, teasing, "with only your head and feet stickin' out. The doctor will git his saw and . . . z-z-z-z-z, he'll saw you in two!"

Ricky laughed. "Will it hurt?"

"It won't hurt half as much to git it off as to keep it on," said Daddy.

Ricky's cast reached from his waist to his toe. He had stayed in the hospital two weeks and would have to go back again to have the cast removed. Now he spent most of his time in the bed in the middle room, where he could see and hear all that went on in the kitchen. But he was tired of lying down and anxious to walk again.

Ricky liked to talk about his stay in the hospital. That evening—the day before Christmas—he began at supper to tell it all over.

"I liked that nurse," he said. "Her name was Miss Whizzengeberry . . . or somethin' like that."

Mama and the children laughed.

"And her hair was so purty, it was *blue* . . ."

"Blue!" cried Mavis. "Do you mean blonde or brunette?"

"Blue!" insisted Ricky.

"BLUE!" repeated Lolly, climbing up on Mama's lap.

"And she brought me two packs of chewing gum and I chewed them both at the same time," said Ricky.

"My! It must be fun to break your leg and go to the hospital," laughed Steve. "Guess I'll let Big Charley's tractor run over *my* leg!"

"*What did you say, Steve?*" An unexpected voice broke into the family chatter. The Hutleys hadn't heard a car honk in front or anybody call—the usual custom to announce an arrival. But suddenly, there stood Mrs. Shands just inside the back kitchen door. She had a large package in her arms. In a moment, the warmth and happiness of the family meal was rudely shattered.

"Did you say you'd like Big Charley's tractor to run over you, too, Steve?" Mrs. Shands' voice sounded icy cold. Joanda shivered.

Nobody could answer a word. But at once, Daddy got up politely and offered Mrs. Shands his chair. She laid her package on the table and sat down.

"I brought you a goose for Christmas," she said.

Still nobody could say a word. They couldn't tell her they didn't want her goose, but they honestly didn't.

"How are you off for groceries, Neva?" Mrs. Shands went on. "Are you having a big Christmas dinner tomorrow? Got a lot of your kinfolk coming?"

"No, ma'am," said Mama gently. "We ain't got much, but we'll make out."

After Mama said these words, things felt a little easier. Steve and Mavis got up from their chairs and hurried out. Joanda picked Lolly up and held her tight.

"How's Ricky's leg coming along?" asked Mrs. Shands, walking into the next room.

It sounded as if she meant to be kind, so Mama told her they hoped to get the cast taken off next week.

"That'll feel good, won't it, Ricky?" said Mrs. Shands. "You're tired of staying in bed, I'm sure. But you won't play around the barn any more, will you?"

"No, *ma'am*," said Ricky.

Mrs. Shands and Mama went back to the kitchen. Joanda felt better.

It was just a friendly Christmas call, after all. The boss-man's wife usually brought something at Christmas time.

As she passed through the kitchen, Mrs. Shands opened the door of the kitchen cabinet. Its shelves were nearly bare.

"Where are your groceries, Neva?" she asked.

Mama's eyes fell. "We're about out," she said nervously. "But we got a little flour and meal and some beans left. And I still got some canned tomatoes and Carnation milk."

"What are you going to have for your Christmas dinner?" asked Mrs. Shands.

"Your goose, I reckon," said Mama with a half smile.

"But if I hadn't brought it . . . ?"

"Great Northern beans!" Mama laughed as she mentioned the well-known brand, the standby of the cotton people.

For a moment, Joanda thought that Mrs. Shands would understand and not be critical. Then she saw a flash in the visitor's eyes and she knew her hope was a vain one. Everything was always somebody's fault and soon Mrs. Shands began:

"Won't you folks ever learn? You made good money from your own cotton and from picking other people's cotton, but what did you do with it? Didn't you buy your winter's supply of flour, meal, lard, sugar, and beans with your cotton money?"

"We got some," said Mama meekly, "but not enough to last out the winter."

"It's true what they say," Mrs. Shands went on. "The cotton farmer lives out of a paper sack. Buying that expensive baloney to eat out in the cotton field; never cooking properly, never taking care of a garden, or eating green vegetables. No wonder you all get sick."

Mama made no comment. Once Mrs. Shands got started, there was nothing Mama could do to stop her.

"Look how you sharecroppers move every year. If a man's no good, he moves because nobody wants him. If he's good and tries to better himself, he won't stay a cropper long—he'll start to work for himself and so he moves, too." She paused. "How will you keep warm this winter?"

"We bought a little coal," said Mama, "but I have to use it to cook with. It won't last long."

"See you don't tear off any of the window or door frames for firewood," said Mrs. Shands sharply.

"Where can we git some wood to burn?" asked Mama.

"We don't furnish firewood," said the woman. "We have no woodland. All our land is in cotton. When that coal is gone, what will you do?"

"I could use that old oil stove," said Mama, "if we could buy coal oil."

Daddy came back in the kitchen. He had been listening on the porch. He had his hat pushed back on his head. That meant he was good and mad.

"I don't guess we'll stay here much longer, Miz Shands," he said.

"Why not? What's wrong?" asked Mrs. Shands quickly.

"A lot of things," said Daddy. "Big Charley's all right to work for. I like him as good as any boss-man I ever had. Big Charley's always ready to do the right thing—if you'd let him, but you won't."

"You sharecroppers are all alike," retorted Mrs. Shands angrily. "You have to move every year—give up the crop and move off. You've been furnished all along, and your crop's not good, so you move off."

"That's about it," said Daddy firmly.

Then Mrs. Shands changed her tone. "You won't leave with the crop still unpicked, will you, Dave? You'll pull the rest, won't you? We're counting on several more bales of cotton this year."

"I don't guess we'll stay much longer, Miz Shands," said Daddy again.

This threat was the only weapon he had. Daddy didn't know where he could get another job, but just to threaten to go, made Mrs. Shands change her tone.

"Charley don't want to lose you, Dave," she said. "Charley says you're a good worker. We're counting on getting at least two more bales . . ."

"It was right good of you to bring us a goose for Christmas dinner," said Daddy, ushering the woman to the door. "We sure do appreciate it."

"I'll send Neva some groceries," said Mrs. Shands. "I never guessed she was that near out or I'd have brought some with me."

All at once Joanda felt sorry for Mrs. Shands. She was backing down so quickly, now that Daddy was showing his proper spirit.

"Oh, don't trouble yourself, Miz Shands, please don't," begged Mama. "We've got a big sack of Great Northern beans and all the kids sure do love 'em. The pot's never empty—I jest keep puttin' more and more beans in."

"I've got some toys for the children out in my car," said Mrs. Shands. She paused, then she added in a low voice: "I'm sorry we couldn't help with that hospital bill for Ricky." It was an apology.

"That's all right," said Daddy. "It was nobody's fault but my own. I'll find a way to pay back J. T."

"Joanda, come out to the car and get the Christmas toys," said Mrs. Shands. "Merry Christmas to all of you."

"Merry Christmas to you and Big Charley," said Mama and Daddy.

Joanda looked at Mama. "Shall I go?"

"Yes, go get 'em," said Mama.

Joanda went to the car and Mrs. Shands handed her a large basket full of packages tied with bright ribbons. The girl tried to thank her, but the words stuck in her throat.

"Merry Christmas!" called Mrs. Shands as she drove off.

"Merry Christmas, Miz Shands!" gulped Joanda. *No matter what they do to you,* she thought, *you have to wish everybody a Merry Christmas.*

She hurried in with the packages.

"What's in 'em? Let's open 'em," cried Ricky.

"Put 'em on the dresser in the front room till tomorrow," said Mama. Then she went on talking to Daddy: "Why do we have to move every year? Where can we find another house?"

"There's plenty of sharecroppers' houses empty right now," said Daddy. "Everybody's been movin' the last few weeks."

"There's plenty houses empty," said Mama, "but not fitten to live in. Seems like I've lived in every cropper house in Oak Hollow and Delta Flats and I know. This ain't near big enough, but it's got a good roof that don't leak. And Big Charley's a good man to work for—the best-hearted boss-man you ever had. You can't go off with part of his crop unpicked. You wouldn't do that to Big Charley."

"Look what he done to me—never offered me a penny to help pay Ricky's doctor bill," said Daddy.

"I been studyin' about that ever since it happened," said Mama. "Maybe he just *couldn't.*"

"Couldn't, huh! Why, Charley Shands is rich, he's made of money," said Daddy. "He couldn't own a thousand acres of this expensive cotton land and have sharecroppers and tenants if he wasn't. He jest didn't want to help me, that's all."

Joanda could keep still no longer. "Does Christmas always mean we gotta move? Are we gonna move right away?"

Mama laughed and that made Daddy laugh, too.

"Not by a long sight," said Mama.

"Not before Christmas, you bet!" added Daddy.

The dog came tearing in, barking loudly. Mavis peeked through the back door. "Where is she, the old sour-puss?"

Steve called, "Is she gone?"

"Yes, she's gone," answered Joanda.

"But she left a lot of presents," called Ricky from his bed.

"Can we come in and put up the tree?" asked Steve.

"Gentle Annie!" exclaimed Mama. "What you got there? A holly tree? What's the ole dead limb for?"

"Ain't no real Christmas trees growin' round here," said Mavis. "So we jest cut a little cypress down by the by-o, and we're gonna fix it up purty."

"Goody, goody! We got a tree!" chanted Ricky. "It's gonna be Christmas after all."

Mavis had bought a roll of green crepe paper at the dime store. She brought it out from its hiding place under the bed, and cut the paper in strips one-inch wide. The children sat down and wrapped it around every branch and twig until the tree was a beautiful bright green. It took a long time. Then they set the tree up on a box in the front room by the bed.

"What will we trim it with?" asked Steve.

"I had a mind to buy some of them shiny balls at the five and ten," said Mama, "but I never thought we'd be havin' a tree."

Daddy looked out the open front door. "I don't see a thing but tin cans," he said, laughing. "Couldn't we tie on a few?"

Joanda looked thoughtful for a moment. Then she said: "I've got an idea. We'll make some shiny things to hang on it. It'll be jest a few little ole play-purties like. Mama, where's the can opener?"

"In the top drawer of the kitchen cabinet, if Lolly ain't carried it off," said Mama. "How you gonna trim a tree with a can opener?" The family laughed.

Mama cleared the supper dishes off the kitchen table and Joanda and Steve brought tin cans in from the yard. With the can opener they cut the round tops and bottoms off the cans. They punched nail holes in the circles of tin and tied strings in the holes to hang them up. Joanda stuck some of the red tomato label pictures onto the rounds of tin. With Mama's heavy old scissors she cut star and heart shapes from the sides of cans.

Meanwhile Daddy had found several ears of popcorn and popped them on the kitchen stove. Mavis strung the popcorn on a long string and they hung that up, too. Soon the tree was sparkling with silver and bright color. Ricky and Lolly clapped their hands to see it. Even with the front door shut and only one window in the dark room, it looked shiny and beautiful.

"It's purty enough for some of our kinfolk to see," said Mama, "if only they lived near enough to come."

On Christmas morning, Mama got up and started the kitchen fire early. She knew it would take a long time to cook the goose, because it was an old one and tough.

"When will we eat?" the children kept asking.

"When the goose gits tender," Mama answered.

The hours passed, the goose simmered and stewed, but each time Mama poked a fork in it, it was still tough.

"We'll wait a little longer, so it will taste a little better," said Mama, and afterwards they were glad they did.

At last Mama got out her linen tablecloth, the one she had when she was first married, and spread it on the kitchen table. She had lengthened the table and put on an extra plate.

"Who's coming, Mama?"

"No one that I know of," she answered. "But when I was a little girl, we always set an extra place at our Christmas table—for the uninvited guest. My mama's idea was that we should be willing to share even the little we had with whoever might come along."

"Even if it was a wicked tramp?" asked Ricky.

"Yes," said Mama.

"Even if it was a bad man, a cattle rustler?" asked Steve.

"Or a cotton rustler?" asked Daddy.

"Yes," said Mama.

"Or an old colored woman?" asked Joanda.

"Or the Queen of England?" asked Mavis.

"Or a ghost?" put in Ricky.

"Or a big old BEAR?" added Lolly.

Mama nodded yes to all. "What a funny meal we'd have if they *all* came!" Everybody laughed.

The dinner was roast goose and beans and stewed tomatoes and bread. Mama put everything on the table and they all sat down. Even Ricky was propped up on a chair. All at once a car horn sounded in front and they could hear a man's voice calling, *Hello! Hello!*" Trouble began to bark.

Daddy went out through the front of the house, almost stumbling over the Christmas tree in his hurry.

"Here comes the big old bear!" cried Lolly, pointing her finger.

The car was an old Ford, and the man at the wheel was old, too, and alone. He had a long beard and was shabbily dressed. They did not know him.

"Are you Dave Hutley?" he asked.

"That's right, sir," said Daddy.

"Is that your wife and family?" The man pointed to the others standing at the door.

"That's right, sir," said Daddy again. "We're jest sittin' down to Christmas dinner, sir. We'd be proud to have you eat with us. We ain't got much, but what we got you're plumb welcome to."

"Thank ye kindly," said the man. "I'm a-comin' right in."

He drove his car up to the porch, and followed Daddy and the barking dog into the house. Daddy went to the kitchen and the strange man came, too. He sat down at the extra place, and after the others were seated, he said a long grace made up of flowery words. Then he took a look around the table, ending with Mama.

"Are you the uninvited guest?" piped up Ricky.

"I sure am!" The old man roared with laughter. "Now I know I'm in the right house, Neva." He winked at Mama.

Mama said, "You're Uncle Shine Morse. I'd a knowed you sooner except for them whiskers. You didn't have 'em when I was a little girl. Children, I told you Christmas is the day when your kinfolk come. This

is my Uncle Shine and yours, too."

Daddy got up and shook hands. "Pleased to meet you, sir," he said.

Soon the plates were piled high and everyone was eating. Uncle Shine ate and talked. He said he had traveled all over the country. He had tried everything. He had peddled lightning rods, painted houses, repaired machines, traded mules, and done all kinds of jobs. Now he was tired of roaming and had come back to Arkansas where he had been born and raised.

"I want to see it again—the cotton country I ran away from."

They talked about Mississippi County and cotton growing. Uncle Shine asked Daddy how he was getting along, and Daddy told how discouraged he was, and how he was always in debt. Mama told how they'd been moving every year since they were first married, and Daddy told about Ricky's accident.

"Seems like everything happens to us," he added.

"Too bad," said Uncle Shine. "Looks like you got to pull yourself up by your own bootstraps."

"Bootstraps?" said Daddy. "I don't wear boots. I wear shoes."

"Looks like you got to learn to *save*," Uncle Shine went on.

"Save what?" asked Daddy. "You mean *money*? We never have no money to save."

"*Save?*" echoed young Steve. "We don't have to save. Any time we want money, Daddy can git it from the boss-man."

"It's as easy as that, is it, Son?" asked Uncle Shine.

"Oh, sure, everybody gits a 'furnish'—even the tenants," explained Steve.

"The boys learn it mighty young," said Uncle Shine.

"He's right, sir," said Daddy. "Steve knows what he's talkin' about."

"And everybody pays eight percent interest on the loan, and they don't even know that's high," said Uncle Shine. "I still say you got to save and git a place of your own."

Daddy laughed. "Once a sharecropper, always a sharecropper."

"Not if you own your team and tools, and git yourself a tractor."

Daddy laughed harder than ever. "You're talkin' about the *moon*," he said. But Mama remembered what Mrs. Shands had said: "If a sharecropper's no good, he moves because nobody wants him. If he's good and tries to better himself, he won't stay a cropper long—he'll start to work for himself."

They got up from the table and went into the front room, where the children opened Mrs. Shands' packages. There was a little bear on wheels for Lolly to pull and a toy tractor for Ricky; a tie for Daddy, socks for Steve, and handkerchiefs for Mama and the girls. There was a sack of nuts and another of oranges and apples.

"Somebody's comin'," said Mama. "I hear a car outside."

The door opened and in came the Burgesses, all of them. Uncle Shine had to be introduced and everybody had to say *Merry Christmas* to everybody else. They all said how pretty the tree was. Then they stood quiet, while J. T. pulled something out of his pocket.

The Hutleys stared with big eyes. It was a billfold. J. T. opened it and brought out a fat roll of bills.

"Money! He's got money!" yelled Ricky from the bed.

"It's a hundred and fifty dollars, Dave," said J. T. "Guess where it come from."

"Must have fell from heaven," said Daddy. "Likely there's a Santa Claus after all."

"It came from your neighbors, Dave," said J. T. "They all knew what a hole you were put in by that big hospital bill, and they wanted to help. Some gave a little, some gave a lot, each gave what he could."

"We only been in this house a year and the folks round here think that much of us?" asked Mama.

"They sure do," said J. T.

Uncle Shine put his arm around Mama's waist.

"They wouldn't a done it, if it hadn't been for you, J. T.," said Daddy in a shaky voice. "Put it right back in your own pocket, to pay yourself back for that hospital loan. If you hadn't a done it . . ." He looked at Ricky.

Ricky was standing up on the bed.

"Now I'm all paid for!" shouted the boy. "Merry Christmas!"

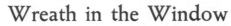

Wreath in the Window

Wreath in the window,
    Pine branches on the door;
Sounds of music playing,
    Dancing on the floor.

Cakes in the oven,
    Pies on the tray;
Oranges and candy—
    A festal array.

White linen tablecloth,
    Candles so bright;
Serenaders coming
    Make music light.

Ripe orange is given,
    Ritual of love—
A symbol of the Gift
    From God above.

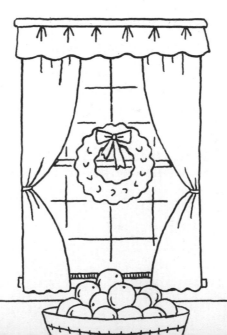

KAYLA'S CHRISTMAS

A Portuguese Christmas

UP IN New England, Cape Cod trusts itself out into the Atlantic Ocean, with high sand dunes along its shores. Behind the dunes, quiet country roads, rimmed with pines, lead away from the sea into purple cranberry bogs. Here, cranberries have been growing wild, their roots deep in peat soil in the marshes, since the days when the Pilgrims landed, and in the centuries since then, have become a staple addition to the American diet.

In the summer, the bogs are drained dry during the growing and picking season. Brown-skinned Portuguese people, known as *bravas*, come to the bogs to pick the berries with wooden scoops. Their children love to come, too. They laugh and shout, fall in the ditches and jump out again, play games, and do little picking. In winter, the bogs are flooded with water which freezes over and makes perfect ponds for skating.

Kayla Santos was a little Portuguese girl, who lived on Aunt Hannah's Lane in a nearby village. She had two brothers, Julio and Roberto, and several aunts and uncles, besides her grandma, who had come from the Isle of Vincent in the Azores, off the shore of Portugal. Aunt Tana and Uncle Diamond lived by the store of Peter Dias. Aunt Pell lived farther away, but she was Kayla's favorite aunt.

Kayla had many friends—Josie Lopez, Sistie Mendez, Izzie Lopez, and among the boys, Joey Mendez and Lukie Lima. They all loved going to the cranberry bogs whenever picking was going on. One day, Kayla did something she shouldn't. Kayla knew all about Grandma's trunk, in which she kept her greatest treasures. Kayla opened the trunk and took out

Grandma's gold pin. It was so beautiful, she decided to put it on and wear it. She wore it to the bog, and there, alas! she lost it.

What a terrible secret for Kayla! She could not tell anyone—until, finally, the burden became too great to bear.

Kayla and her brothers went out to cut their own Christmas tree. "This one is the prettiest," said Kayla.

She pointed to a small spruce tree. Roberto took his axe and chopped it down.

Kayla and the boys were in the woods by the beach. The ground was coated with snow. It was very cold, with a hard wind blowing. The breakers were high, topped with whitecaps. The sky was dark and it began to snow again.

Kayla stamped her feet to keep warm.

"Guess we won't go in swimming today," said Julio.

"No," said Roberto. "But skating maybe—tomorrow. All the cranberry bogs are frozen solid now."

"Hurry, let's go home," said Kayla. "I'm so cold!"

She ran on ahead through the snow. The boys followed, carrying the tree between them. They walked through the woods path, crossed the highway, and came to the corner by the store of Peter Dias.

Sounds of music came from inside the store. Roberto peeped in the window.

"Uncle Diamond is in there, playing his guitar," said Roberto. "Peter Dias has his accordion and Lukie Lima's father his mandolin."

"Uncle Diamond gave me his old accordion," said Julio. "He says I'll soon be as good as he is."

"Father says he'll get me a violin," said Roberto.

The children passed Aunt Tana's house. She waved to them from her back door. At the next house, Aunt Pell called to them to come in. She gave them cookies to eat. They warmed their hands by her stove.

Then they hurried on with their Christmas tree. All the way down Aunt Tana's Lane, people were getting ready for Christmas. Some put wreaths in their windows or pine branches on the door. Sounds of music came from some of the houses. Everybody was in festive spirit.

At home, Mother and Grandma had worked hard all day. Special dishes were cooked for a real Portuguese Christmas. In the kitchen, the table was already set. The best white tablecloth had been taken from Grandma's trunk. Candles were ready to light.

Soon everything would be ready for the evening serenade. The house looked beautiful.

Roberto and Julio set the spruce tree in the corner of the living room. Kayla hung shiny balls and strings of popcorn on. She thought it was very pretty. Mother brought out American gifts and laid them under the tree.

Father came home and everybody dressed up in his Sunday best. Then they sat down and waited.

"I hear them coming!" cried Kayla.

She went to the front window to look out. Above the pine trees across the road, she could see the moon rising in a deep blue sky. Sounds of music came closer and closer.

Their serenaders were going from house to house. Not a single Portugese home in the village would be missed. All were celebrating Christmas, the day of Christ's birth.

"Here they come! Here they come!" cried Kayla. She danced on tiptoes, she was so happy.

Father opened the front door and called in a loud voice, "Welcome! Welcome to this house on Christmas!"

Five men stood outside. They carried musical instruments. Their leader stepped up and said, "Now we enter this house with the good will of God. Blessings be upon this house at Christmas time!"

The men came in, shaking the snow off their feet. Some boys came in, too. The men tuned up their violins and guitars. Julio brought his accordion. They played and sang carols in Portuguese.

Then the men turned to Peter Dias. He was appointed to say the prayer. It was an old traditional prayer from the old country. He sang the prayer instead of saying it. When Grandma heard it, the tears rolled down her cheeks.

Then Father invited the guests to the table.

Kayla had never seen the table so beautiful. With the lighted candles, it was like a feast. There were three cakes, several pies, bowls of apples, oranges, and candy. There were other special Portuguese dishes.

Father said, "Here is the gift, the Christmas gift!"

He gave Peter Dias an orange. Peter put it in the bag he carried. It was the custom for the home-owner to present a gift, no matter how small.

The men and boys crowded round the table with the family. They helped themselves to food and drink. They danced around the table

"Thank you, thank you" called the Santos family.

On the afternoon of Christmas Day, the children went skating. Lukie Lima's father came after them in his car. He took the Lopez children and the cousins, too. The car was very crowded. They drove to one of the cranberry bogs near the ocean, where the ice was best. The boys took wide shovels and brooms and brushed the snow off.

It was Kayla's ill-fated bog. She hated to think of the trouble that had come to her there.

Kayla had received new skates for Christmas. She changed to the skate shoes and started to skate. At first she felt awkward. But soon she got used to the new skates. Soon she was skating as fast as anybody.

The boys played hockey with sticks and a ball. The girls played *Crack the Whip*.

Izzie Lopez was the leader. She shouted:

> *"Crack the whip and let it zip,*
> *Do not fall, roll like a ball!"*

She swung the line of five girls as hard as she could. They went sailing over the ice, Kayla on the tail end. Faster and faster she went, at last tumbling down. The girls laughed and teased her.

Now the boys stopped playing hockey. Up on shore, they built a fire. They brought wood from the pine woods near by. They fed the fire and it burned brightly. They crowded round to warm up.

The girls came over, shivering. They took sandwiches and apples from their coat pockets and ate. Cold winds blew in from the ocean, but they scarcely noticed. Hands and toes were cold, and noses were red. But skating on the bog was fun.

When the fire died down, they ran back to the ice for one last round of skating. Boys and girls formed in one long line. Julio, the oldest and strongest boy, cracked the long whip.

"*Crack the whip and let her zip!*" he shouted.

Away went the children, sailing over the ice. Kayla was in the middle of the line. Suddenly her ankle turned and down she went! The line broke. Two parts of the whip sailed away and left her.

Down on the ice in a huddle she lay. A sharp pain shot through her ankle. She tried to get up, but couldn't. She unstrapped her skate. She decided to walk. She took her boot off and stared at her ankle. It had begun to swell. It felt very sore. She must have twisted it.

She started to pick up her boot, then let it fall from her hand. She stared at the ice. She saw something shiny just below the surface. She could not make out what it was.

The girls came running up.

"Why don't you get up?" asked Cousin Nancy.

"Come on—we're going home," said the Lopez girls.

Sistie Mendes and Cousin Marcella tried to help Kayla up.

"I've hurt my ankle," said Kayla. "I can't walk on it."

Sistie called the boys. Julio and Roberto came over. But Kayla did not ask them to help her.

"Look!" she cried. "Look, Julio! There's something under the ice—frozen in. What is it?"

Julio got down on his knees. He took his knife out of his pocket. He used the largest blade to dig into the ice.

"Golly!" he said. "You've found something all right!"

"Once I found a can of sardines under the ice," said Nicky Lopez. "Somebody's lunch at cranberry time! It had never been opened. When we thawed it out, we ate the sardines. They were good, too."

"What do you think it is, Julio?"

Kayla hardly dared breathe. She did not dare hope. She leaned heavily on Sistie's shoulder. She forgot about her ankle.

Julio kept on digging. All the children were excited. "What is it?" they asked.

Julio brushed the ice off and held it up.

It was Grandma's gold pin which Kayla had lost months before!

Kayla's eyes shone as she took it in her hand. "Oh, I knew I'd find it!" She hugged it tight. "A Christmas present for Grandma," she said.

When she reached home, Lukie Lima's father had to carry her in the house and put her on the sofa.

"She sprained her ankle and will have to stay off it for a while," he explained.

But nobody listened to him. Nobody looked at Kayla's ankle. All they could see was Grandma's gold pin in the little girl's hand.

Kayla gave the brooch to Grandma and was happy again.

City Santa

Ding-a-ling-din!
Ding-a-ling-din!
As you pass by
Drop your pennies in.
Food for the hungry,
Clothing for the poor;
Each gift brings God's blessing
And blesses you more!

There are no reindeer,
There is no sleigh,
Santa gave them all away.
Now he stands over there
At the street corner where
The people throng
The whole day long.

Over the rooftops—
How could he go?
He has no airplane,
No helicopter, so
He just stands there
Too lazy to go anywhere.
He stands on the corner
And rings a bell—
When you hear it—it's Santa!
You can always tell!

Ding-a-ling-din!
Ding-a-ling-din!
As you pass by
Drop your pennies in!

CHRISTMAS ON MACDONALD STREET

A City Christmas

A BIG CITY in the east was a maze of crowded streets. Most of them were numbered from south to north, but MacDonald Street ran at an angle crossing the others, so it had a name all its own. Once it had been a residential area of substantial homes three and four stories high. But the neighborhood had changed and become shabby. Small stores had taken over ground floors, and most of the buildings had become cheap apartments. Soon, in the relentless course of so-called progress, they would all be torn down, the people moved out, and new and taller buildings, planned for purposes yet unknown, take their place.

MacDonald Street was a busy thoroughfare. Because it was a shortcut from one corner of the city to another, it carried a heavy traffic load, especially of business and commercial cars and trucks. The streets and sidewalks were seldom cleaned. The street was dirty and shabby and noisy, but to many people, it was home. Those who lived there, people of many nationalities, knew each other and were friendly and helpful.

All the apartments were walk-ups, without elevators. Front doors opened out onto brownstone stoops, with railed openings at one side and stairs to basements below, where the landlord usually lived. Children loved to play on the stoops and stand there and talk to each other.

"Yes, I saw Santa Claus," said Kathy.

"Where?" demanded Leo.

"Downtown," said Kathy. "Mom took us over to Riverside first, to the Parkview, to see about gettin' a job . . ."

"Did she get one?"

"No," said Kathy, "but they told her to come back again. They've got plenty of waitresses right now, but when one of them leaves, they'll give Mom a chance. Mom's girl friend Sadie works there—she'll let us know. Then we took the subway down to Thirty-fourth Street."

Leo looked at her soberly.

"And you saw Santa Claus down there. On the street corner, I bet. How many Santas did you see?"

"Oh, a lot!" cried Kathy, her face lighting up. "There was one on every corner and they kept ringin' a little bell . . ."

"Did you give Santa something?" asked Leo.

"I had some pennies in my purse," said Kathy, "and I put 'em in the pot. And Mom put in a dime."

"That's not a real Santa Claus," said Leo.

"I know that," said Kathy. "It's just an old man dressed up. He puts on a wig and a beard and a red suit trimmed in white."

"It's the Volunteers of America," said Leo, "beggin' for money. Those Santa Clauses don't bring kids anything for Christmas."

"Yes, they do," said Kathy. "They take dinners to poor people and toys to their children, one of them told us so. I was glad to give him my money."

"O.K.," said Leo.

Kathy Ryan, ten, and Leo Delgado, two years older, were standing by the stoop in front of Kathy's apartment house, on a side street uptown. They were both in the fourth grade at P.S. No. 193, a block away, but there was no school now because of the Christmas holidays. Kathy lived on the top floor of her apartment house with her mother and two little brothers.

Leo lived across the street. His mother was dead, so he lived with his father and his grandmother and his Uncle Tony. Their apartment was second floor front. All the apartment houses on MacDonald Street were old brownstone fronts, which had once been fashionable residences but now were shabby, and cheap because they were shabby.

They were crowded with large families of many children. In the summer all the stoops were filled with people, and the fire escapes had potted plants on them and lines of clothes drying. But now that cold weather had come, they were practically empty. It made the whole street seem lonely, in spite of the noisy traffic roaring by.

"Then we went to see the REAL Santa Claus," Kathy added.

"Where was that?" asked Leo.

"Up on the seventh floor of Magee's Department Store," Kathy said. "Oh, it was terrible getting there . . . So many people, everybody pushing and shoving and growling and scolding . . . Once Larry and Donnie let go of Mom's hands and nearly got lost, and a man was trying to carry a Christmas tree over our heads and bumped into us, and the Christmas music was so loud and jazzy I could not hear what Mom said and people kept dropping packages . . ."

"You call that fun?" asked Leo, grinning.

"No, but it was the only way we could get there and Mom had promised the kids," said Kathy. "Going up the escalator, I had to hang onto Larry and Mom had to carry Donnie."

"And what did you see when you got there?"

"SANTA CLAUS, of course!" said Kathy. "It said Make-a-Wish-Land on big signs up on the walls and Santa Claus sat on a high throne and on the steps going up were candy canes as big as trees, and two big reindeer, real ones, leaning over his shoulder and nodding their heads! Their eyes moved, too. And on all the Christmas trees there were bright ornaments that shone like silver and gold and kept moving back and forth. Oh, it was wonderful! You should see it, Leo!"

"Oh, heck!" said Leo. "That's for the birds!"

"They even had big birds hanging from the ceiling with shiny bright feathers and tails in all colors, that opened their bills and sang . . ."

"I thought you went to see Santa Claus," said Leo.

"We did," said Kathy. "He was the nicest Santa of them all, much nicer than those on the street corners. His long white beard was all curly and he had real fur on his red suit, but . . ."

"But what?" asked Leo.

"We had to wait a long, long time in line because there were so many children. The others were asking for typewriters and electric trains and drum-major sticks and transistor radios and propeller guns, and one even asked for a piano! Santa kept saying: 'You be a good girl—or boy, now. I'll try to get it for you, sweetheart!' He was sweet as pie and patted the little kids on their heads and kept saying, 'Sure, I'll bring it,' 'Sure, you'll get it,' 'Move along now . . .' By the time we got there, he was cranky and cross. Then it was our turn and Larry went up and kicked him and Donnie screamed his head off, he was scared to death! They forgot to tell him what they wanted . . ."

"Just as well," said Leo.

"So *this* Santa dumped them both off his lap and said, 'Take these brats away!' and it made Mom so mad, she grabbed the boys by the arms and left and kept sayin', 'I could just murder him!'"

"And you?" asked Leo. "Did you ask Santa for what you want?"

"No," said Kathy. "I'm too old for that. I don't want anything for myself, just something for my little brothers."

"You didn't talk to Santa, then?" asked Leo.

"I should say not! *I hated him!*" cried Kathy. "He wasn't mean to the other kids like he was to my little brothers." Then, remembering, she added: "But it was worth it—it was all so beautiful with the fancy lights and trees and trimmings and all. The store was fixed up so pretty and there was Christmas music playing, but there were too many people . . . you couldn't see very well . . ."

"Better stay at home, then," said Leo.

"Yes," said Kathy. "But Mom wanted to give the little boys a treat. That's about all they'll get."

"Yes?" asked Leo.

"Yes!" said Kathy.

"We don't get much for Christmas at our house, either," said Leo. "It's not Christmas any more without Mom."

Across the street, a second-story window flew up, and an old woman put her head out and started screaming.

"LE - O! LE - O!" she called. "Where you at, LEO? Come home!"

It was Leo's grandmother. He heard her calling and the next minute he was gone. He dodged through the traffic to the other side of the street. He had to see what Grandma wanted. She never left him to himself very long. She always had to keep an eye on him.

Kathy thought for a minute. She felt sorry for Leo. Somehow it would be easier for Kathy to get through Christmas, knowing that Leo's would be empty like hers.

Just then Mom came out the front door. Mom always looked nice, Kathy thought. She was young and pretty, with curly brown hair, and she

Larry and Donnie with her and told them to stay with Kathy.

"What you doin', hon?" she asked Kathy.

"Nothin'," said Kathy, "just waitin' for somethin' to happen."

Mom laughed. "A fire engine, maybe?"

Kathy shook her head. "The boys would like that. Or a police car. But nothin' ever happens around here."

Mom said she was going to the dime store a few blocks over.

"Don't let the boys see me when I come back," she said.

"O.K.," said Kathy. She knew she was going to buy their presents.

Kathy thought of her father, whom she could hardly remember. He had been killed in the war overseas and all Mom had left was an enlarged picture of him, with his officer's cap on, and his medals on his shoulder. No wonder Mom's had a tough time, she thought. If only she could get that waitress job . . .

Donnie and Larry squatted on the stoop and began to play with their battered toy trucks. They played quietly a long time. Three little neighbor girls, Gertie, Mamie, and Ruthie Hornberger, came over and played a while, too. A cold wind began to blow, so they buttoned their coats tight. Kathy leaned on the railing and wondered when Mom would get back.

Then all of a sudden, a shiny black Cadillac drove by and stopped at St. Cecelia's Convent Chapel, a few doors away. The driver, a young woman, opened the rear door and brought out two baskets of blooming red carnations and started for the chapel door.

Kathy and the little girls ran down to see. Larry and Donnie came, too.

"Gee!" said little Gertie. "Look at all the pretty flowers."

"They're *real*, too!" Kathy caught her breath. "Not like those in the dime store."

Kathy had not seen many freshly-cut, blooming flowers in her life. The only ones she could remember were those at Leo's mother's funeral. The thought made her sad. Then she spoke to the young woman.

"Lady," she asked, "is somebody dying?"

The lady looked at the eager little faces and was shocked. Did fresh flowers mean only *death* to them?

"No, children," she said kindly. "These flowers are to be put on God's altar for Christmas. They are to make people happy!"

"Oh!" said Kathy, with a smile. "I'm glad nobody died."

She called the boys, and started back home. Looking ahead, she saw Mom coming back with parcels in her arms. Kathy smiled—at least there would be *something* for the boys.

A garbage pick-up truck stopped to load cans of trash. Kathy let the boys watch it. After she saw Mom go quickly in, she waited a while longer.

Then she said, "Come, boys, it's time to go home."

On Christmas Eve, it began to snow. Mom put the children to bed right after supper and told them to go to sleep. In no time at all, she woke them up again and helped them get dressed. They put on their wraps and left the apartment just before eleven o'clock. They walked down the street for midnight Mass at St. Cecelia's.

It was wonderful to be up in the middle of the night. On the way home, everything looked different, almost beautiful with the covering of white. Kathy pointed to the stars overhead. They were twinkling brightly, and one was brighter than all the others. The people who lived on the ground floor, the Ferrantes, had put green wreaths tied with red ribbons in their front windows. They looked pretty by the light of the street lamp.

Larry saw them first. "See!" he said. "It's Christmas!"

Upstairs in the apartment, they went back to bed again and slept late. In the morning, Mom had turned the radio on and started breakfast. While they were eating, a knock came at the door. Surprised, Mom told Kathy to run and see who it was.

"It's a delivery boy!" Kathy called to Mom. "He's got a big basket full of groceries. Did you order some things to be delivered, Mom?"

"No," said Mrs. Ryan. "It's a mistake. He's got the wrong address."

She came to look over Kathy's shoulder. A big card with a Christmas wreath on it was tied to the handle of the basket with a red ribbon. Mom stared.

"It's not ours," she said gruffly. "Take it back. We never ordered any stuff from Dominico's!"

The boy read the label over again.

" '*Mrs. Katherine Ryan, 795 MacDonald Street, fourth floor front!*' " he read. "Ain't that you?"

"Yes," said Mom. "But there's some mistake. It's not for me."

"Yes it is, madam," said the delivery boy. "I can't wait around all day." He walked into the kitchen and set the heavy basket on the table. "It's yours, all right. *Merry Christmas!*"

Then he was gone.

Kathy looked at Mom, and Mom looked at Kathy.

"Somebody sent it . . ." said Mom.

"Somebody wanted us to have Christmas," said Kathy.

With trembling hands, Mom opened the envelope and drew out a card. It had a picture of Jesus in the manger on it. Inside was a hand-written message:

"To wish you a Merry Christmas and God's blessing, from St. Cecelia's Mothers' Club."

Mom flopped down on a chair and cried. Kathy put her arms around her. "We've got good friends, Mom," she said.

"And I haven't been to their meetings but once or twice," said Mom. "How did they ever find out I need help so bad?"

By this time, the children had unpacked the basket and spread every-thing on the table. It was a complete Christmas dinner—a huge turkey, with vegetables and sweet potatoes, celery and olives, lettuce, tomatoes, and a big mince pie. Each separate item was a marvel.

"Well, we'll have a fine Christmas dinner, I can see that," said Mom. She tied on her best apron and added, "I've got a big job ahead of me."

"Mom!" said Kathy, coming up and whispering. "Can I ask Leo to come over and eat with us? He said he don't have any Christmas at his house since his mother died."

"Why, yes, of course!" said Mom, happily. "With those toys I got at the dime store for the boys, we'll have Christmas after all."

Kathy ran to look out the front window.

"There he is now, out on the sidewalk. I see him!" she cried.

She threw the window open, put her head out and called, "Leo! Leo!" But the traffic was heavier now and it was raining hard, so it was impos-sible to make him hear. "LEO! LEO!" she kept calling.

Suddenly Leo heard. He dashed across the street between cars and yelled back, "What you want, Kathy?"

"Come on up and eat dinner with us! We've got a great big turkey!" called Kathy.

"O.K.," said Leo. "I'll be over soon. Got to go back and tell Grandma first."

The kitchen was full of sweet smells and the little boys were playing happily with their new toys, when Leo came over. He was dressed in his best suit and had a tie on his white shirt. His curly black hair was neatly brushed.

"Saw a police car go south just now," he said.

"Something wrong?" asked Kathy.

"Probably some drunks," said Leo. "Maybe they celebrated too much last night. Now they got to sober up in jail."

"Your pop and Uncle Tony get the day off?" asked Mom.

"No," said Leo. "Some big boats came in this week. That means lots of unloading for the men. Christmas don't mean anything down at the river docks. They told Grandma they might get off before night, but wasn't sure."

Leo's father and Uncle Tony were longshoremen, who worked hard every day and often at irregular hours. They were strong men and enjoyed their heavy work. Pop was very proud of his *gaff*, or longshoreman's hook.

"And Grandma, what does she do all day on Christmas?" asked Mom. "Won't she come and eat with us, too?"

"Naw, she stays all day long at St. Cecelia's praying," said Leo. "Nothing could tear her away but an earthquake."

Mom and Kathy laughed.

Soon the Christmas dinner was ready and everybody sat down to enjoy it.

"I wish I could have invited Sadie Greenbaum, my girl friend," said Mom. "But she had to work today. So many people like to eat out in restaurants on holidays. The Parkview does a big business of Christmas."

The meal was delicious, down to the very last crumb. Kathy was glad she had asked Leo over. After he ate, he had fun showing the boys how to use their new toys. One was a toy airplane and he flew it all over the room. Mom had a new red sweater for Kathy and she showed it to Leo proudly.

Outdoors the rain had stopped and the sun came out. It shone through the front windows and lighted up the floor through the thin curtains. It brightened the whole day. Everybody was happy and contented.

Then suddenly, everything changed.

Loud footsteps were heard in the hall, a key turned in the apartment-door lock, and in rushed an angry man, waving a gun in his hand. The children began to scream.

Leo dropped the toys and came to the door. Kathy and Mrs. Ryan stood up, astonished. Leo faced the man squarely and would not let him go any farther.

They all knew who it was—Mr. Doyle, the landlord.

"You, Kate Ryan, you owe me a month's back rent and you better pay right now or I'll . . ." He dodged Leo, rushed to the corner where the boys were playing and kicked their toys with his foot. He saw Kathy's old doll in its carriage, both of which her daddy had got for her on his last Christmas at home.

"Toys and dolls you've got a-plenty, I see!" he shouted, still waving his weapon. "You got money for dolls and toys . . ." He pointed at the remains of the roast turkey on the table, "and you can buy Christmas turkeys to feed to all the kids in the slums . . ." He glared at Leo. "But you got no money to pay your back rent." He stopped his ranting for a minute. He had run out of breath.

Mom tried to speak.

"I've only missed this last month," she said quietly. "The little money I had I needed for household expenses and a few toys for the children for Christmas. I'll pay you out of my pension check the first of the year, I promise. And I'm trying to get a job, too. Can't you wait, Mr. Doyle?"

"Wait! Wait! You just want me to wait till you're good and ready. . . ." He began to shout again. "I want my money, or I'll break up everything in this house . . ."

Leo, black-browed and red-faced, could stand no more. He rushed up to Doyle, to reach for his gun and stop him. Doyle stumbled over a chair and fell to the floor, still shouting and screaming. Leo jumped on the man's prostrate body.

Mom turned to Kathy. "Call the police!" she cried.

Kathy ran to the front window, opened it, and leaned out.

"Po - lice! Po-lice!" she screamed. "Come quick!"

Across the street, two big strong men happened to look up. They heard the girl's cries over the din of the traffic.

"Why, it's Katie Ryan's girl!" said Pop Delgado to Tony.

The men were just coming home from the river dock.

"Katie's in trouble." Pop turned to Tony. "Get the police. I'll go see what's up."

The next minute Pop was across the street. He rushed to the fourth floor, taking the stairs three steps at a time, and came to the Ryan apartment. The door was open and he stalked in.

To his surprise he saw Leo, his son, sitting astride Old Doyle, the landlord, and pounding him heartily. Leo pointed and Pop looked. On the floor in a corner lay Old Doyle's pistol. Pop walked over and picked it up, then he threw it down again.

"It's a toy—he ain't got a real one," said Pop. "He was just puttin' on a show!"

Mrs. Ryan and Kathy and the little boys were huddled in a corner, their arms around each other, white-faced and frightened.

"He didn't even knock," Leo told his father. "He just came in, shouting that he wanted his money. He said he would break up everything in the house and us, too."

Heavy steps came up the stairs and in walked Uncle Tony and a policeman. Pop Delgado explained what had happened, and the men led Old Doyle, still angry and sputtering out the door and down the stairs. Leo went with them.

"He's good and drunk," said Pop Delgado. "They'll lock him up!"

The children ran to the open window and looked down to the street. They saw Old Doyle loaded into the police wagon and carried away. The Delgados went back home.

"We never even had a chance to thank them," said Mom.

She and Kathy dried their tears, closed and locked the door, and began to put things in order. No serious damage had been done.

Mom looked at Kathy with a twinkle in her eye. "Was it just yesterday I heard you say nothing ever happens around here?

Kathy laughed. "But where's the fire engine?"

Mom put the rest of the turkey and the leftover food into the refrigerator.

"We'll have enough food to last us all week," she said with a smile.

Just when they sat down to rest after an exciting afternoon, the telephone rang. Mom went to answer. "Now who can that be?"

She talked a few minutes, then she turned to Kathy. "It's Sadie."

Kathy's heart skipped a beat. Would Sadie have good news? She had to wait until Mom hung up the receiver to find out.

Mom was smiling from ear to ear.

"I've got a job!" she said. "At the Parkview! It pays the most and the tips are high. Sadie says they were sorry they didn't take me on last week, when I went for the interview. They liked me and put me at the top of their list. They've been so rushed over Christmas, they want me to start right away . . . tomorrow! Good thing I scrimped and got me that nice new uniform!"

Kathy rushed up to Mom and gave her a big hug.

"I'm so glad!" she said. She knew how hard Mom had worked to keep the family together ever since Daddy died.

"But, Mom," she added. "What about Larry and Donnie? School starts again right after New Year's Day, and we can't leave them here alone."

"Grandma Delgado will baby-sit," said Mom. "I've already asked her.

She gets tired of doing nothing at home all day long, except feeding her three men. She likes kids—she'll be good to them."

"She yells a lot, Mom," said Kathy.

"That doesn't mean a thing," said Mom. "Grandma's used to yelling at her men-folks. She's got a heart of gold. Don't worry—a little yelling won't hurt Larry and Donnie. She'll make 'em mind. I'll take them over before I go to work, and you can bring them home, after you come from school."

"Then I'll cook supper and have it ready," added Kathy.

A knock came at the door and there was Leo. He had his old clothes on and his face was smudged and dirty.

"Come see what I got, Kathy!" he called.

Kathy grabbed her coat and rushed down the long flights of stairs behind him.

On the front stoop stood a big Christmas tree. It looked a little misshapen and bedraggled, but it still had some garlands of tinsel and some shiny balls fastened to it.

"Where did you ever find it?" gasped Kathy.

"On a garbage truck down the street," said Leo with a grin. "Some folks there had their Christmas last night and threw it out a little while ago. I was right there, coming back from the Police Station, and I grabbed it. When I got home, Grandma made me put my old clothes on."

"What did they do to Old Doyle?" asked Kathy.

"Just locked him up," said Leo. "They'll keep him locked up till after New Year's Day, they said. He always drinks too much and makes trouble for his tenants. They know all about him."

"Oh, Leo! Mom's got a job!" cried Kathy. "She starts tomorrow, at the Parkview. Sadie Greenbaum called to tell her."

"Gee, that's great!" said Leo. "Nice Christmas present for your mom, after the way Old Doyle spoiled things."

"What are you doing with your tree, Leo?" asked Kathy.

"Come and see," said Leo.

He carried the tree on his shoulder and led her down the street. The little Hornberger girls and other children followed. They came to the little yard by St. Cecelia's Church. The chapel was at the back of the yard, with an iron fence and gate across the front. It was open to everybody. The yard itself was cement, without grass or trees. In one corner lay some old bricks and cement blocks.

Leo went in and set his Christmas tree up in the middle of the yard. The children brought bricks and blocks, and Leo used them to brace the tree at the bottom, so it would not fall over.

"It's beautiful!" cried Kathy. "A real Christmas tree!"

The children joined hands in a circle around it. They sang in thin, piping voices:

> *"Oh, Christmas tree, oh, Christmas tree,*
> *How lovely are your branches!*
> *In summer sun or winter snow*
> *A dress of green you always show—*
> *Oh, Christmas tree, oh, Christmas tree,*
> *How lovely are your branches!"*

Three nuns, with large black and white headdresses and long black robes, came out the chapel door, watched and listened. One of them came forward and said, "Bless you, children! And a very Merry Christmas."

A city sparrow flew down and sat on the topmost branch of the tree. Kathy turned to Leo.

"We had a nice Christmas, after all," she said. "Didn't we, Leo?"

Leo grinned. "We sure did."

Blow Blow

Blow, blow, icy winds blow!
Bearing your burden of heavy snow;
Creep, creep, little snowflakes, creep,
Drifting over the valleys deep,
Over the fence,
The grass and the stone,
Over the little house
Standing alone—
Cover them all with a blanket of white,
Cover them softly all through the night.

Blow, blow, icy winds, blow!
Pile up your drifts of cold, cold snow.
Soft, soft, little snowflakes, lie still
On sloping prairie and rising hill.
Over the grasses,
The lambs and the sheep,
Over the cattle
Huddled in a heap,
Cover them all with a blanket of white,
Cover them softly all through the night.

THE CHRISTMAS PROGRAM

A Prairie Christmas

THE GREAT prairies of the Dakotas are not flat, as one might suppose. They roll and tumble like the great waves of a mighty sea. Treeless sloping mounds are covered with native sod, once green, but in summer browned by wind and sun, and in winter covered by great drifts of white, cold snow. The great prairies stretch far away to the distant horizon, under the big blue bowl of the sky. It is said of the prairie people that they have "the far look in their eyes," from looking, looking, looking, always scanning the distant horizon.

The people who live on the prairies are rugged stock. They have to be to survive, for the climate is fierce rather than kind, and it taxes all their instincts for survival. Blizzards trap herds of cows for weeks, keep families in isolated farmhouses stranded, and often keep children snowbound in isolated schoolhouses, sleeping on the floor in their school clothes. The one-room schools have two small rooms added on, called "the teacherage," where the stalwart teacher, who would be unable to travel back and forth from even the nearest town, must live throughout the school year.

At Oak Leaf School, the nearest home was three miles away. No school bus could travel the frozen, drifted, snow-covered prairie roads. How did the children get to school? In Daddy's jeep or truck, or on horseback, and when the horse could not get through, on foot, walking ahead of the horse, kicking the path open.

All these hazards and dangers were taken in stride. The children accepted them as daily routine—they knew no other way of life. Sleeping on the school floor for two or three nights, or for as long as two weeks was just a usual way of waiting out a blizzard. There were no telephones, because no lines could be strung or kept in repair. So parents at home had to wait patiently for their children's return, hoping that the teacher had not let them start out in the raging storm, to be buried under the snow. These conditions were still true in 1950.

The Johannes Wagner family and their neighbors were "Russian Germans," whose parents had gone from Germany to live in Russia for a generation, and then come to this country. To them Christmas was an important festival, although dependent on the hazards of the weather. Putting on a Christmas program at Oak Leaf School was the height of fun for the children.

"Only nine more sleeps till Christmas!" exclaimed Delores.

"Oh, I just can't wait to see what I'm gonna get," said Fernetta. The two girls put their heads together, giggling.

"Jacob drew my name," whispered Delores. "Tell me what he's got for me."

"No, sir, it's a secret," said Fernetta. "But it's something nice."

"Please, Fernetta, please." Delores jumped up and down. "Tell me."

But Fernetta wouldn't. "I bet that old Emil Holzhauer will give me a fly-swatter or something crazy. He's loco!"

The girls burst into peals of laughter.

"Boy! Won't he look purty dressed up in whiskers?"

Emil's head came round the curtain. "Boo!" he shouted. "I'm gonna be Santa Claus and scare the little kids." He held his mask up in front of his face, and the girls tried to snatch it off.

The Oak Leaf children were getting ready for their Christmas program, and had already drawn names for the exchange of gifts. The first snow had long been forgotten. Other snows had come in late November and early December. The prairie was white now, surrounded by snow-topped buttes. Snow was an everyday experience, while overshoes and heavy wraps had become daily necessities.

The program was to be held in the evening, to make it easier for the parents to come. The children worked hard to get ready. They made a big fireplace out of cardboard cartons, and pasted red lined crepe paper on to look like bricks. Darrell made a base for the Christmas tree, bought by Emil long ago in November and kept carefully hidden in the barn until now. Chris Bieber and his wife, Vera Mae, who had no children, brought a battery and a string of lights for the tree. The boys helped string the lights on while the girls stood and admired.

The desks were turned around to face the back of the room. Jacob and Wilmer Sticklemeyer stretched the curtain wire across, and hung the stage curtains on it. This made it possible to use the teacherage kitchen for a dressing room. The Biebers and the Hummels brought lanterns, one for kerosene and the other a gas lantern with a mantle, which made a very bright light.

Evening came all too soon. The people arrived early, as soon as evening chores were done. There were the Hummels, Sniders, Engleharts, and the Sticklemeyers, who had children in school, and the Burgards, Hunstads, and Becklers, whose children were grown up now. All the families

Merry Christmas!
Dec. 25, 1948

brought their younger children, who were soon running around the schoolroom. The last ones to arrive were Johannes and Minna Wagner.

"So much to do," complained Mrs. Wagner. "My work, it never gets done." The other mothers nodded their heads in agreement.

"Is it going to snow?" asked Mrs. Englehart. "Ain't it about time for a real good storm?"

"Ach no! We want no storms this winter," said Mrs. Pete Hummel. "I remember a storm once . . ." The talk went on and on.

At eight o'clock, Miss Martin herded the children into her bedroom to put on their costumes.

"I brought my records," said Ruby Englehart. "I got two records to play."

"Delores, has the phonograph come?" asked Miss Martin.

"Darrell drove to town to get it," said Delores. "He'll be here any minute. Ruby's got 'Jingle Bells' and 'Silent Night.' "

Delores was to be Mrs. Santa Claus. She put on her mother's old black silk dress and a little lace cap of Grandma Wagner's. She stood in front of Teacher's mirror in the kitchen and rouged her cheeks and painted her lips. Then she peeped through a hole in the stage curtain, but Darrell wasn't there.

"Jeepers!" she cried. "There's Uncle Gustaf."

He hadn't said a word about coming. He had probably brought Christmas presents for everybody. He always gave her something nice. She wondered what it would be this year. Oh, it was exciting not knowing what anybody was going to give you.

Fernetta Sticklemeyer came out of Teacher's bedroom dressed as Mother Goose and Ruby Englehart as a fairy queen.

"My mama went to Mobridge last week," Delores whispered to Fernetta. "She brought home a lot of packages and she hid them. I know right where they are—on the top shelf of Mama's closet."

"I got two records already," chimed in Ruby. "My uncle gave them to me."

"Go away," said Fernetta. "We're sick of hearing about those old records of yours. Who cares, anyway?" She turned to Delores. "What do you think is in them?"

"I shook one and it gurgled," said Delores. "Something runny."

Fernetta closed her eyes shrewdly. "Shampoo, maybe? Or a perfume set?"

"I hope it's perfume," said Delores. "But maybe it's for Lavina and not for me. Mama says I'm not old enough."

"She want you to stay a baby?" asked Fernetta.

Delores peeped through the hole again. "Why, there's Darrell. Look, Fernetta, he's talking to Katie Speidel and Norine Schmidt. I bet Uncle Gustaf brought them out from town. They're my best friends—in town, I mean."

Miss Martin sent Peter Hummel out to bring Darrell back of the curtain, but he had no phonograph. "The man wouldn't lend it without a down-payment," said Darrell, "and I didn't have any cash."

"Then you'll have to sing, children," said Miss Martin. " 'Jingle Bells' is the first number."

Hans and Fritz Holzhauer, Emil's older brothers, came to manage the stage curtain. They had graduated from the eighth grade several years before and liked coming back to their old school.

When everybody was ready, the program began. The curtains were pulled back on both sides, and the children sang "Jingle Bells." Several recitations followed and then it was time for the play *Santa Claus at Home*. In the middle of the performance, Hans Holzhauer dashed back to the kitchen and said, "I'm having trouble. Where's a safety pin?"

"Go look on Teacher's pincushion," whispered Delores.

The curtain had come unhooked from the wire and was sagging badly. Hans hooked it up with a safety pin and the play went on. At the end, the curtain went shut without a hitch and everybody clapped.

After the program came the refreshments. The mothers were always willing to bring food to school, and all had contributed. Everyone ate candy and nuts, oranges and cookies. *Halvah* was popular. The Sticklemeyer family brought twelve pounds of the sticky, taffylike candy, all in once piece like a large loaf. Mrs. Sticklemeyer sliced off generous chunks and passed them out. Every child old enough to reach out a hand was eager for *halvah*.

"In the old days we made it ourselves," said Ruby Englehart's grandmother. "Now everybody buys *halvah* at the grocery store."

"What's it made out of, anyhow?" asked Uncle Gustaf Wagner. "Sunflower seeds? It tastes like machine oil to me."

The grown-ups laughed.

"Oh, it's got crushed sesame in it—that's a grain from the old country, and corn syrup, sugar, egg whites, and vanilla," explained Grandma Englehart.

"Whatever it's got in it, it sure tastes good to me." Pete Hummel thrust a large bite in his mouth.

"Oh, not so fast!" cried Grandma Englehart. "That's not the way to eat *halvah*. My mother she make me eat it so—first a big bite of bread, then a little bite of halvah, then bread again. That way it goes not so fast. It's better for the stummick, too."

The others laughed. The room was filled with warmth and friendliness, with good talk and laughter. The children were shrieking and romping with the school dog Spike. Grandpa Englehart was telling a story:

"Never vill I forget! When I turned over that first strip of prairie sod, I remembered that no man ever touched it before, since the day the good Lord had made it. I tell you then I vas a little scared—and that old Indian watching me, too. Never vill forget vat he said—just three words: 'Wrong side up.' Then he turned his back and walked away."

Nobody said anything. Suddenly the light in a lamp on the window sill flickered. A gust of wind blew in through the broken pane. The lamp flared again and went out. Mrs. Sticklemeyer screamed, and her youngest, little Alvin Calvin, ran to her and began to cry.

Pete Hummel quickly moved the lamp to a safer place. Then he went out the front door, and in a minute was back.

"Hey, folks!" he shouted. "We're gonna have a white Christmas all right. It's snowing hard."

"Snowing—no!" answered the women.

"Looks like a storm comin' up," Peter went on. "Guess we better be gettin' on home."

"Don't tell me it's goin' to be a blizzard," cried Mrs. Sticklemeyer. "I ain't got Adolph's red flannel underwear out yet!"

The others laughed nervously, getting up from their chairs.

"You can't go yet," said Miss Martin, trying to shout above the din. "Santa Claus still has a little work to do. The children haven't had their presents. We drew names and . . .'"

"Santa Claus! Santa Claus!" cried the children. "We want our presents." "What you got for us, Santa Claus?"

Emil Holzhauer, wearing his red suit and bearded mask, put his head out from behind the stage curtain and cried: "Hey, wait! Don't go yet. I ain't had my show. What you think we made this crepe-paper fireplace for? Don't you know I got to climb down the chimney and scare the little kids?"

Just then the curtain wire broke and came down. The dog Spike barked and pulled at it, and this time a safety pin was no help at all.

"Come on, we gotta go home," called Pete Hummel again.

"Go home?" cried the women, startled.

Mrs. Englehart had a plate of cookies in one hand and a dish of nuts in the other. Mrs. Hummel was passing out fruit, and Mrs. Wagner was cutting another large three-layer chocolate cake. The refreshments were not half over.

Darrell jumped on a chair in the center of the stage. "Santa Claus hasn't come down the chimney yet," he shouted. "Wait a minute, please..."

But no one was listening.

Delores ran to her mother. "Don't let Papa go yet," she said, with her mouth half full of *halvah*. "We've had lots of snowstorms before and we always got home. I want to see what Jacob Sticklemeyer's got for me . . ."

But Delores could not stop her father. Johannes Wagner said in a loud voice: "There's a storm coming up. Better get home quick, folks."

"Can't we eat first?" cried the boys.

"Don't wait to eat," said Sam Englehart. "Take your food and go home."

"Leave the refreshments for Teacher!" laughed Uncle Gustaf.

"Oh, no!" cried Miss Martin. "I'm going to Aberdeen for the holidays. Everything here will get frozen. Take the food with you. Take everything with you. Maybe some of you will take my canned goods, so it won't get frozen while I'm gone."

Like leaves scattering before a wind, the pleasant gathering broke up. Quickly the children thrust presents into each other's hands and in Teacher's. Dishes and food, wraps and small children were collected by the women. Caps, coats, scarves, and four-buckle overshoes were hastily put on. Each family took a carton of Miss Martin's canned goods and everybody started to go, calling: "Merry Christmas! Merry Christmas!"

"I want a present from Santa Claus!" wailed little Christy Wagner. Minna wrapped him, screaming, in a blanket and Johannes threw him up over his shoulder.

"Delores, hurry now, get on your wraps. We're going," called Mama Wagner. "Ach, now, what is the matter? What are you crying for?"

"That crazy old Jacob, he didn't give me much—just a stationery, without even pictures on it," sniffed Delores. She opened the small box and showed the note paper to her two girl friends from town, Katie Speidel and Norine Schmidt, who were waiting for Uncle Gustaf to come.

Miss Martin came running out into the hall and touched Johannes Wagner lightly on the arm. "Mr. Wagner," she said. "We're about out of coal . . . Do you think you could bring some? Before I get back?"

"Yah, yah, sure!" replied Johannes. "I see about it right away, quick, tomorrow. I been too busy to take care of it before."

"You going to town tonight, Miss Martin?" asked Mrs. Wagner.

"Yes," said Miss Martin. "Gustaf said he would take me. I'll leave everything as it is and throw a few things in a suitcase. I'll get the fast train to Aberdeen tomorrow."

Delores saw the worried look in Miss Martin's eyes fade away, as Papa promised to bring the coal. The girl tied her scarf tightly under her chin and buttoned her coat. Miss Martin was still standing there. She had her pretty blue silk dress on, the one she wore to church on Sundays, but no sweater, no wrap, and the front hall was cold with the door standing open. Impulsively, Delores ran to her and threw her arms about her.

"Good night, Miss Martin," she whispered. "Merry Christmas. I hope you have a nice vacation." She followed her parents out into the stormy night.

After the truck engine started, the cab was warm and shielded them from the wind. Only a little snow was falling, but it might get worse in an hour's time. As they rumbled away, Delores looked back and saw the lights in the schoolhouse. She was glad that Uncle Gustaf would drive Miss Martin safely to town.

"Will it be a blizzard, Papa?" asked Delores.

"What? This?" Papa Johannes laughed. "This is nothing."

But it was a blizzard, after all, the worst in several years, even though Papa pretended to make light of it. The men were away day and night, getting hay for the cattle. While they were gone, little Christy became so sick and Mama so worried, that Delores decided to go to town for medicine. It was the third day of the storm, so she knew it was almost over. There was only one way to get to town—on horseback, on Old Nellie.

It was a long hard trip through heavy drifts to the Hunstads, where Delores had to leave the horse. Old Nellie could go no farther. Then on foot, she trudged all the way to Uncle Rudolph's, found him there luckily, and rode with him in his jeep to town. They got there just before the stores closed, and she was able to buy a bag of groceries and get the medicine for Christy. She spent the night with sister Lavina in her trailer-house, and next morning Lavina gave her a small Christmas tree for Mom. On Christmas Day she made her way home again.

"Here comes our Christmas tree girl!" Mama met her at the door and gave her a tight hug.

"Lavina sent the tree, Mama," said Delores. "Ain't it pretty?"

"Ach! You are home safe again," said Mama. "I was sick with worry when you did not come home last night. Poor Christy, he could hardly breathe. I ran the steam kettle all night for his cough. I never once took my clothes off even."

"I got the prescription filled just before the drugstore closed."

"Good," said Mama. "Soon he will be better."

"Jeepers! Is the house ever hot!" exclaimed Delores. "Must be, Papa brought the coal."

"Yah, at last," said Mama. "They got stuck three times and had to walk back to town to get Schweitzer's wrecker to come pull them out. They took half the load over to Biebers', so Vera Mae could have a warm house for Christmas, too."

"And the boys?"

"They finally got a load of hay to the barn, and the cattle came in," said Mama. "Poor kids—that is work for men, not for boys. That Ozzie, he's only nineteen—just a kid, too."

"Mama!" exclaimed Delores, remembering. "Papa's got to get coal for school, too."

"Yah, I told him," said Mama, "and he said there is plenty time for that."

"He better not wait too long," said Delores.

Soon Papa and the boys came tramping in.

"Merry Christmas!" shouted Papa. "They tell me it's Christmas!"

While Mama was preparing and roasting the duck for Christmas dinner, Delores set the little evergreen tree on the sideboard in the front room. Darrell hung shiny balls and tinsel on it. Mama brought her packages out from their hiding place and laid them under it. After dinner, Mama got Christy out of bed and held him on her lap to see the tree. Delores heated the iron and pressed her wild-rose dresser scarf. It was all she had to give to Mama.

"Jeepers! Is the house ever hot!" cried the boys.

Once the lignite coal in the furnace was well started, it made the house too warm. The family threw off sweaters and coats.

"It's like summer, hey?" Papa chucked Mama under her double chin.

"Come on, let's open the presents," begged the boys.

"What Santy Claus bring me?" asked Christy. "Candy bar?"

The gurgling package was perfume, just as Delores expected. She got a new blue sweater and a pocketbook, too. Mama gave her a kiss for the dresser scarf, and said wild roses were her favorite flowers. Ozzie and the boys got plaid work shirts and Christy a toy dump-truck. After admiring all the presents, they all ate *Kaffeekuga* and drank hot coffee.

Then came Grandma Wagner's treats—a paper sack for each grandchild which contained one orange, one apple, nuts, cookies, Russian peanuts, a candy bar, and a popcorn ball. Grandma sent a new tie for Papa Johannes and for Mama a pretty pincushion crocheted on the wishbone of a chicken.

At the last minute, Papa tossed a small box into Mama's lap. When Mama opened it, they all gathered round and gasped in astonishment. It was a pretty gold wristwatch on a gold-chain bracelet.

"Well, I never!" exclaimed Mama. The kiss she gave Papa was a resounding smack. "Look at me here now, with this! A wristwatch! Don't that beat the Dutch! And I thought I was lucky to get *coal for Christmas!*"

A Knock at the Door

A knock at the door,
    Open and see!
La Christine *comes*
    For you and for me.

A long robe he wears,
    Crown of moss so grand;
Sack on his shoulder,
    Switch in his hand.

Any bad boys here
    Who lie and steal?
He whacks his switch
    For them to feel.

Any good boys here,
    Who always obey?
For them from my sack
    I give toys today.

Then out the door
    He's gone from sight,
Leaving firecrackers popping
    All through the night.

LA CHRISTINE COMES

A Bayou-French Christmas

Down in the Delta country, where the Mississippi meets the sea, water covers the land, and the land is more water than land. On one of its waterways there stands a little village, with a footpath on the levee. All the houses face the water, each with a dock in front. The people are French and speak more French than English. They travel by boat and fish from their boats and from wharves and *pirogues*. A pirogue is a hollowed-out canoe.

Fish is their food and their means of living. By boat they go into the swamps to catch alligators and to gather Spanish moss hanging from the trees. The children play on the docks, while their fathers mend their nets and bait their lines, and their mothers sit on benches on the levee, gossiping and doing their mending.

In one of the houses lived the Jules Durand family. There was Papa Jules and Maman, big brother Ambrose and big sister Eulalie, then Suzette in the middle, and after her, three little brothers, Joseph, Jacques, and little Noonoo. There was also Grandmere and many aunts and uncles. But the family was not too big to take in an important new member, Marteel, a homeless Indian girl. When Suzette heard that Marteel had no home, no mother, no bed to sleep in, she had to bring her home with her, although Maman did not like it much—at first.

Papa Jules was not a good fisherman. He did not even have a boat of his own. He had no houseboat so he could not go trapping muskrats in the wet prairies as his neighbors did. He had a very good excuse—a bullet in his back, and when his back got stiff and sore, he had to rest.

Some people said he was lazy, but Suzette knew it was not true. She was always loyal to her beloved Papa!

The arrival of cold weather brought thoughts of *le jour de Noël*, Christmas. All the children became excited, wondering what their Santa Claus, whom they called *La Christine*, would bring them. Not only did *La Christine* come, but a visitor as well, a Mr. Johnson of Minnesota, and it was because of him that Marteel, the Indian girl, who had a habit of running away frequently, returned. How happy Suzette was, to have Marteel come back for Christmas!

"If only we had a houseboat!" cried Maman. "If only Jules had any kinda boat of his own!" The tears rolled down her cheeks. "Jules, he never make no money, him," she said, sadly. "He too lazy to go trappin'! He want to loaf round all the time and do not'ing. Each time he went trappin' before he got shot, he came back with not enough money to pay for w'at we eat while we gone. He never have none left over. We never get no silk dresses, no shiny shoes, no phonygraph to make music."

Suzette put her arms round Maman's waist. "W'at matter dat?" she said, bravely. "Me, I don't want no silk dress, no shiny shoes, no phonygraph."

"Better times, they come," said Grandmère, "if only you hold up your chin. Jules, he get stronger and next year he go trappin' and get rich, mebbe."

"Mebbe," repeated Maman, bitterly.

"W'y you not go trappin' muskrat in the prairie?" she demanded, when Papa Jules came in. "Your brothers they go, the neighbors they go, ev'body go but you."

"Can't *swim* to the trappin' grounds," said Papa Jules. "Can't go trappin' without boat and supplies. And my back, where the bullet is, it get stiff and sore, when I go in damp, wet place like the prairie."

"Plenty excuse!" sniffed Maman. "That bullet in your back, it not'ing but rheumatiz."

Papa Jules shrugged his shoulders, picked up his gun, and whistled for his dogs. "Me, I fish crab, I fish fish—when they bite—and when they don't, I go huntin'. Make two-three cent today, we eat tomorrow."

"For months now, you en't make half a dollar," said Maman.

But all the scolding did no good. Papa Jules continued in his lazy ways, absent more and more often from home, hunting, thus, however, keeping the family well supplied with game.

Days passed. One morning the faucet on the rainwater cistern was frozen and had to be thawed out.

"Cold weather it bring *le jour de Noël!*" cried Maman, smiling.

"Our Maman, she won't let us forget Christmas, no?" said Papa Jules, with a laugh. "It good, that. *La Christine*, our Santa Claus, must get a hearty welcome. All we need is plenty money to spend!"

"Plenty money!" sniffed Maman. "W'at you t'ink? You so lazy, mebbe we git two-three cent to spend for Christmas."

Papa Jules said nothing. He only smiled.

"Nonc Lodod and Nonc Moumout and ev'body come home from the trappin' grounds," cried Suzette, happily. It would be wonderful to have

Beulah and Doreen and all their neighbors back, though only for a few days. Suzette's eyes brightened as she thought of *le jour de Noel* and counted the days. Then her face fell. If only Marteel would come! She wanted no presents for herself. She wanted only Marteel.

The day before Christmas, Papa Jules came into the kitchen laden down with mysterious packages and on top of them, two fat ducks. Maman eyed him suspiciously, so he explained.

"Me, I killed a big buck and Eugène, he shipped it to market and give me a good price for it."

"How much?" demanded Maman.

"Oh, two-three cent!" laughed Papa. Everybody else laughed, too. "Now, en't you glad I go huntin' every day? En't you glad that big buck make Christmas for us? Oh, yes, here two fat ducks I brought down— cook 'em for dinner tomorrow."

The mysterious packages disappeared from sight. Maman forgot all her worries and set to work. She loved to cook and Christmas dinner was worthy of her best efforts. There was chicken and oyster gumbo, fluffy white rice, roast duck, white cream tarts, and a layer cake. Tante Toinette and Nonc Moumout came to help eat it, drink wine, and enjoy the fun.

The meal had hardly begun when little Noonoo came running in. "A big new lugger with a red sail!" he shouted, pointing out the front door.

"Now who comin'," cried Maman, "just when we ready to sit down!"

Papa Jules hurried out to find the lugger already moored to the end of his wharf. The children followed at his heels.

"Good day, sir!" said an immaculate gentleman, stepping ashore. He stretched out his hand.

"Monsieur Johnson!" cried Papa Jules, delighted, taking the hand in both his own. "From Minnesota! My good frien', how fine to see you again. And just in time for Christmas dinner. Where you been so long?"

"Lost!" replied Mr. Johnson. "I expected to be back in Minnesota in time for Christmas, but I got lost in those confounded marshes. My maps are no good. They show only about one-quarter of the waterways. I never knew what a labyrinth Louisiana is! You go down one stream or bayou or coulée, only to find yourself in another. I've been going round in circles for days!"

"How you find yourself again?" asked Papa Jules.

"One day, in a deserted spot, I ran across an Indian girl who spoke good English and she directed me to Bayou Barataria. Then I knew where I was."

An Indian girl! Suzette's heart missed a beat. But the men went on talking and she had no chance to ask questions.

"Come in! Come in, take Christmas dinner with us!" cried Papa Jules, bubbling over with hospitality.

"But it will be troublesome for your wife . . ."

"Not at all! Not at all!" cried Papa Jules. "She t'ink it an honor to serve you her roast duck."

Mr. Johnson could not refuse the cordial invitation, after his dreary days on the bayous. The visit was a gay and happy one. After dinner, Mr. Johnson told of his gold-digging adventures. He told of visiting all the places where Jean Lafitte was said to have buried his treasure. He told of exploring Barataria Bay, Grand Isle, Grand Terre, and many adjacent islands and shores.

"And w'at you find, my frien'?" asked Papa Jules, with a sparkle in his eye.

"Nothing! Not a single gold-piece for all my pains!" answered Mr. Johnson, laughing.

"Then you not rich, m'sieu'?" asked Maman, wide-eyed.

"Poorer than when I started," replied Mr. Johnson, "for I've spent all my money."

"It good, that!" murmured Maman.

"You mean, good that I am poor again?" exclaimed Mr. Johnson.

"Oh, no, m'sieu'," cried Maman, in great confusion. "I only mean, it good . . . that Jules, my husban' . . . he not go with you!"

"So it goes! So it all the time goes, yes!" cried Papa Jules. "Many men, they fools before. They have risked much and lost everyt'ing. But w'at a fine fable, is it not? And w'at a great man—Jean Lafitte! Always the French fisherman of Barataria, they will do him great honor."

"And digging for gold," added Mr. Johnson, "is the greatest sport of all."

Suddenly a loud knock came at the door. Suzette opened it, giggling, and a strange, half-grown figure stepped in, dressed in a long, loose woman's wrapper. His cheeks were bright red, smeared over with elderberry juice, and he wore a crown of Spanish moss wrapped round his head. He carried a long switch in his hand and a loaded burlap sack over his shoulder.

"Here comes *La Christine*!" he announced. "Any good children here? Any bad children?"

Joseph and Jacques, Suzette's little brothers, stepped boldly forward. "We good! We good!" they cried eagerly.

"No, you bad, and I switch you!" *La Christine* chased them round the room.

Little Noonoo, frightened, ran and hid behind Maman's chair. *La Christine* approached quietly, looking in all directions. "Any good leetle boy here, name' Noonoo?"

"Here! I . . . me good!" cried Noonoo, peeping out.

"I got somet'ing for you," said *La Christine*, " 'count of you been such a good boy."

He opened his big sack and took out a little red wagon for Noonoo. Then he gave a monkey-on-a-stick to Joseph, a tea set to Suzette, a baseball bat to Jacques, and a bottle of perfume to big sister Eulalie.

Last of all he brought out firecrackers, which all the boys pounced upon and which were soon set off to a noisy popping.

Papa Jules turned to Mr. Johnson. "It not Christmas in Louisiana without firecrackers."

"It sounds more like Fourth of July to me," said Mr. Johnson, laughing.

During the excitement, *La Christine's* wreath and wrapper fell off, and there was brother Ambrose, red-faced and merry, in the midst of the fun.

There were no gifts for the elders—no phonograph, no silk dresses, no shiny new shoes—but no one mentioned the fact.

At last it was time for Mr. Johnson to go. The family all went out to the wharf to watch his departure. Mr. Johnson thanked his friends for the happy Christmas, shook hands all round and stepped aboard the lugger. He put his head inside the cabin and spoke to a passenger there: "I thought you were going ashore here. Isn't this where you wanted me to bring you?"

A small dark-skinned figure, with tangled hair and ragged clothes, came out of the cabin and stepped from the lugger to the wharf. She moved forward confidently, never once doubting her welcome.

"That's the girl who guided me back to civilization," said Mr. Johnson, as the boat shoved off.

"Marteel!" cried Suzette. She ran to her side and took her hand. "You come back for Christmas?" she whispered.

Marteel nodded, smiling. "Christmas—w'at dat?"

No one else spoke. Mr. Johnson's lugger moved slowly out into the bayou, while the family watched. When it had passed round the bend, Marteel ran to Maman and reached up her arms. But the look on Maman's face made her drop them again.

"W'at you come back for?" inquired Maman, coldly. "En't I tole you to go back to the woods and stay there?"

"White girl, me," said Marteel. "Suzette's sister, me."

"There she goes again . . ." began Maman.

"It Christmas, Clothilde!" began Jules, gently. "En't your heart big enough?"

"Have you forgot w'y we shoo her off?" demanded Maman.

Grandmère had been watching the look on Suzette's face. "We can't shoo her off on Christmas, Clothilde," she said, softly. "And look how dirty she is . . ."

"W'at she needs is a kind maman to give her a bath," added Papa Jules. "A kind maman . . ."

Suddenly a loud squawking was heard coming from back of the house.

"Run, Suzette, see w'at that is," cried Maman. "Somet'ing been killin' my hens. Bring in the eggs while you there. I make omelette for supper."

Suzette darted over the levee and into the yard. Marteel looked at Maman's face again and then, without a word, followed Suzette.

That summer, several rows of okra had been planted down the length of the garden. Their prickly dead stalks reached from the shed to the picket fence which separated the yard from the marshy field beyond. Suzette saw the squawking hen between the rows and chased her.

Suddenly she stopped short in the path. "O-o-o-o-h!" she screamed.

There at the end of the row stood a wildcat, ready to pounce on the hen. "Eee-ee-ee-ee!" hissed the animal.

The hen got away and came toward her. Suzette stood staring. Her breath was gone. She couldn't scream now.

"Run back!" The sharp words hit her ear. A hand touched hers and Marteel was beside her.

Suzette looked down in the path in front of her. The wildcat was there now. She saw Marteel's bare, brown foot on the struggling animal's head. On the fence beyond, she saw three more wildcats with angry eyes, hissing mouths, and spreading whiskers.

"I hold him. You run!" Marteel's words came again.

Then Suzette saw the animals on the fence leap down upon the hen in the path and roll over fighting. The air was filled with flying feathers, but there was no more squawking. She screamed and ran.

The screams brought Papa Jules and Ambrose, with their guns, running. The screams brought the dogs, Roro and Toto and little Poo-poo, barking. Bam! Bam! Bam! Bam! The shots followed one after the other in rapid succession. The wildcats turned and fled, with the dogs at their heels.

Afterwards, no one knew exactly how many wildcats there had been, but one thing was sure. At least two of them would never leap the fence again.

Marteel sauntered slowly toward the house, where the family waited by the back doorstep.

She looked up at Maman with a glint in her eye. "That hen, she won't never lay no more eggs," she announced.

Maman said nothing. She turned to Suzette and listened as she began to tell about Marteel's bare foot on the wildcat's head.

Suddenly Maman took the Indian girl in her arms, held her tight and wept. "And I tole you to go back to the woods!" she wailed. "Marteel! My leetle Marteel!"

Papa Jules looked on, surprised.

Maman tried to explain: "She en't not'ing to me—but she's got herself wrapped round my heart and me, I can't turn her loose."

"*Joyeux Noël!*" said Grandmère, softly. "Merry Christmas!"

A Bright Light

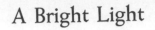

Out in the piney woods
　　Under the trees,
The scent of pine needles
　　Is sweet on the breeze.

Out in the piney woods
　　The sun sets red;
And then slowly sinking
　　Leaves darkness instead.

Out in the piney woods
　　Gleams a bright light;
A house door stands open,
　　A gay tree in sight.

Out in the piney woods,
　　Lights on a tree;
Children crowd round it,
　　Happy to see.

Out in the piney woods,
　　A dream come true;
Children find Christmas,
　　Their faith renew.

THE CHRISTMAS FAKE

A Backwoods Christmas

THE RIDLEYS' house stood all alone back in the great piney woods. From the blacktop highway, a shady road wandered in and out around pine trees and palmettos to get to it. Sometimes trucks and wagons got stuck in the loose sand and had to be jacked up before they could be pulled out.

Two old live-oak trees stood near the house, with broken branches and streams of Spanish moss hanging. The unpainted house, built of vertical battens, had turned a dull gray from the ravages of wind and weather. It had a porch across the front and four rooms inside. Under the house, several wild hogs were rooting. Tangled, torn curtains hung at the windows and the front door stood wide open. Blocking the entrance, lay three hound-dogs outstretched. Their names were Trixie, Patches, and Jerry. Daddy insisted they were good watchdogs, but Mom said they were lazy and good for nothing.

Letty was ten, the oldest, Mike seven, and little Punky three. Besides Mom and Dad, there was Mom's sister, Aunt Vi, who spent most of her spare time with them. Mom didn't like living out in the backwoods so far from town, but the owner let them rent the house for almost nothing, so she tried to make the best of it.

The days were still as hot as midsummer. The only way any one could tell that winter was coming was by the shortness of daylight. The sun seemed to set earlier every night. Just as soon as the big red ball slid down into the horizon, the dark dropped down like a heavy black curtain. The short days meant December, and December meant only one thing to the children. Christmas came to them in hot weather, not in cold. Christmas was green to them, never white. Having lived all their lives in the sunny south, they had never seen snow.

"How many days till Christmas?" asked Mike.

Letty, his sister, answered. First it was ten, then only seven, and now it was only one. Christmas was tomorrow.

"I want a doll and a buggy to ride her in," said little Punky.

"I want a bicycle and a BB gun and a football," said Mike.

"Forget it!" said Letty. "You won't get 'em."

"How do you know?" asked Mike.

"I asked Mom," said Letty. "She said there's no money for presents. I asked her if we could have a tree, and she said no money for a tree, either."

"I'll ask Santa Claus," said Mike.

Letty stared at her brother. Mike was seven now. Did he still believe in Santa Claus?

"Mom said she's gonna take us to town to see Santa Claus," Mike went on. "He's coming in a helicopter, landing right in City Park. I'll ask him for what I want."

Letty felt sad. She hated to tell Mike the truth. Let him believe in Santa as long as he could.

"Don't you remember when the man came and took our TV away?" she began. "'Cause Daddy only made the first payment?"

"Yes, and I fought him," said Mike. "Then he told us we could have it back after . . . Daddy got a job."

"Daddy got a job," said Letty, "but it's way over on the east coast. He can't even get home for Christmas. We never got the TV back either. Don't you know that, Mike?"

"Yes, but we will," said Mike. "Daddy told me so, the last time he was home."

"He's got a job, but still there's no money for anything," said Letty bitterly.

"I know that," said Mike. "So I'll just ask Santa Claus . . ."

It was hopeless, so Letty said no more.

Mom said they could all go to town that afternoon to see Santa Claus. She made them wash their faces and necks and ears and arms and put their feet in the tin tub to get them clean. She got out clean clothes for them and they put shoes and stockings on. Letty's dress was patched, but it held together.

The Ridleys did not have a car. Daddy drove to his new job on the east coast with a neighbor who worked there, too. They left early Monday morning and did not return till late Saturday.

It was only a mile to town, not too far, except when Punky went along and got tired and had to be carried. Today Aunt Vi came by in her Ford and picked Mom and the children up. Aunt Vi had a job in an office in town. She typed letters for a real-estate man. She was having a few days off for Christmas.

When they got to town, Mom went with Aunt Vi to the beauty shop. Aunt Vi was to get a permanent, and Mom had to go to the supermarket for food. The children jumped out at Main Street. "Meet me at the bench at the corner," said Mom, "after Santa Claus leaves." It was too early for Santa Claus now, so Letty took Punky in the dime store. Mike saw some boys and went off with them.

How festive the little town looked! The light posts along the street were trimmed with tinsel and red paper bells. All the stores had Christmas decorations in their windows. From several, loudspeakers were blaring Christmas music. There were many shoppers going in and out. Everybody was happy because Christmas was coming.

Letty started down Main Street, pulling Punky by the hand. Punky broke loose and dashed on ahead. So Letty had to skip along fast to keep up. Inside the store, Punky ran down the aisle and picked things off the counters. Letty made her put them back and slapped her hands.

Letty had two dollars of her own in her pocket. She had earned it baby-sitting for the Boyers. They had four little ones under six and she often sat with them. She went to the jewelry counter. She wanted a pretty brass pin to wear on her shoulder. There were so many it was hard to choose. They were only twenty-five cents. If there wasn't going to be any Christmas at home at least she could buy herself a present. She'd still have $1.75 left to help pay for that new coat she needed.

"Is that your little sister?" asked the clerk.

Letty heard a child crying, but did not look up.

"Yes," she said. "She bothers the daylights out of me. Keeps me runnin' my legs off. I get mad at her. I take her by the arm and jerk her."

"Better watch her now," said the clerk. "She's helping herself to a doll. Guess she's too little to know you have to pay for things in here."

"Do you know what I do to make her mind?" asked Letty.

"No," said the clerk, "but you'd better do it quick."

"I spank her," said Letty. "Not when my mother's around, of course. I spank her with my hand—hard too!"

She rushed over to Punky, took the doll out of her hand, and spanked her. Punky screamed and stamped her foot.

"Now you keep still," said Letty, "or I'll take you home."

Letty dragged her back to the jewelry counter.

"Does spanking make her better?" asked the clerk.

"Well, no," said Letty. "The more I spank her, the more I have to spank her."

Punky ran back to the doll counter. She picked up the doll again. "She really wants that doll," said the clerk.

"Oh, she wants everything she sees," said Letty. "She's always saying 'gimme, gimme . . .'"

Punky called out: "I want it, Letty, I want it . . ."

"Well, you can't have it!" answered Letty. She bent over the jewelry counter again. Should she get the flying bird or the butterfly? The brooches were all so pretty, she could not decide which one she liked best.

"Has she got a doll at home?" asked the clerk.

"No," said Letty. "She's had dozens, but she breaks 'em all up."

"She ought to have one," said the clerk. "Why don't you buy that doll for her? Then maybe you could keep her quiet. A little girl like that needs a doll to love and play with."

Letty looked up startled. What business was it of the clerk's? She opened her purse. In that moment, she had an important decision to make. She looked across to the toy counter, where Punky was holding up the doll. It was just a cheap one. She saw its price tag—49¢. Then she looked down at the butterfly brooch in her hand.

"I'll take this," she said. She handed the clerk a quarter.

The clerk made no comment. She put the brooch in a small paper bag and rang up the money.

Letty rushed over and jerked Punky away from the toy counter. Punky began to cry. "I want a dolly . . . I want my mama . . . I wanna go home . . ."

The clerk came over and spoke again: "Do you ever read her a story? Or take her for a ride in her little wagon?"

"What wagon?" Letty stared at the clerk. "Punky hasn't got any little wagon."

"She'd be a pretty little girl," said the clerk, "if you'd wash her face."

"She bothers the daylights out of me," said Letty.

Out on the sidewalk, Punky was still crying. Letty leaned over and wiped her tears away.

"Do you want to see Santa Claus?" Letty asked.

"Yes," said Punky.

"We'll go see Santa Claus, and you can ask him for a dolly," said Letty. "Tell him you want a great big doll as big as a baby . . ."

Punky smiled. "As big as a baby," she said.

The little City Park was crowded now, with children of all sizes and ages. Men from the Jaycees were herding them into a long line.

"Get in line! Take your turn!" the men shouted.

Overhead, a loud buzzing sound could be heard. The children's eyes all turned toward the sky. There, coming closer and closer, was a helicopter. It slowed up, then came straight down in a roped-off open spot. The door opened and Santa Claus stepped out. He was very fat, dressed in a bright red suit, and had a white mustache and a long white beard. The children screamed with delight.

Letty looked over the crowd and finally spotted Mike. She called to him. Mike made his way over to her and they waited their turn, holding Punky tightly by the hands. Once Letty lifted Punky up so she could see Santa Claus.

The children in the line asked for everything under the sun from bicycles, typewriters, and pianos to parakeets, rabbits, and turtles. The line moved slowly toward the big fat Santa Claus.

"We're next!" said Letty, pushing Mike forward.

Mike never forgot for a minute.

"I want a bicycle, a BB gun, and a football," he said in a loud voice. Santa patted him on the back.

"I'll do what I can for you, Son," he said and shoved him along. "Who's next?"

Now it was Punky's turn. She stared at the big fat man and his white whiskers, half-frightened.

Letty leaned over. "Say what you want, Punky," she prompted. "Tell him you want a buggy and a doll . . ."

"I want . . ." began Punky. "I want *a great big doll as big as a baby*!"

Santa laughed. "You be a good girl now," he said, "and I'll try to get it for you, Honey."

Then he turned to Letty.

"You're too old . . ." he began.

"I want a watch!" said Letty emphatically. "Not a Mickey Mouse one —I'm too big for that. A real one, I want this time. That's the only thing I want. I don't care if I get candy or anything else—just a wristwatch!"

Santa eyed her coldly.

"What if you don't get it?" he said.

Letty shrugged. "I'll be satisfied with what I get, even if it's nothing. That's all I can do, I reckon."

But Santa was not listening. He had shoved her quickly aside. He was beaming and smiling and making rash promises to all the children coming behind.

When they got out of the crowd, Letty said to Mike, "Oh, I hate that guy!"

"Who?" said Mike.

"That fool of a Santa Claus," said Letty.

Mike's eyes opened wide.

"Why, he's going to bring us . . ." Mike began ". . . the things we asked for!"

"Oh, no, he's not!" cried Letty angrily. "He's tellin' lies—to all the kids in town, makin' them believe he'll bring them anything they ask for!"

Mike's face turned white. "You mean . . .?"

Punky began to cry.

Letty did not stop there.

"Santa Claus is just a fake—a big Christmas FAKE!" she said. "I don't believe anything like that. Three years ago I knew it. I got up that Christmas-Eve night to see Santa, and it wasn't him. It was Grandma, I saw her—not even Daddy—puttin' presents out."

The sparkle in Mike's eyes faded, as they filled with tears.

Then suddenly Mom and Aunt Vi came up and Aunt Vi told them where the car was parked.

"Did you tell Santa what you want?" asked Aunt Vi.

"Yes," said Punky. "He said he's gonna bring me a dolly."

"I asked for a bike," said Mike, soberly, "but he don't have to bring it if he don't want to."

Letty lagged behind.

She looked around sharply. Mom and Aunt Vi had no packages under their arms and she saw none in Aunt Vi's car. They had gone shopping but had bought nothing. Santa Claus was just a fake, and so was Christmas. Now she was sure of it.

"I'm gonna walk home," she told Mom.

"O.K.," said Mom. "Better get there by suppertime if you want anything to eat."

Letty walked slowly home, with a heavy heart. She hated the decorations on the street now and the sound of the Christmas music. What good was it all? There would be no Christmas at home. Mom had told her so. The only promise Mom made was, if Dad got the day off, they might eat out and go to a show. Whenever they ate out, Letty took two hot dogs and ice cream. What fun was that?

Letty came to a vacant lot, where Christmas trees were being sold. A young man came rushing out and tried to urge her to buy a tree.

What good was a Christmas tree?

Then Letty stopped in her tracks. Maybe . . . maybe they could have a tree, at least. It would be better than no Christmas at all. There was a box of shiny balls and a string of electric lights left over from a couple of years ago. She knew just where they were, on the bottom shelf of the kitchen cupboard.

Why not have a tree . . . with lights on it?

It would be better than nothing. Especially if there were no presents. Punky would like the pretty lights if she couldn't have a doll-baby.

But the trees were not cheap.

"Two dollars each," said the man, holding one up.

"It's too big," said Letty. "Have you got a smaller one?"

The man found a smaller one, but it was two dollars, too.

Letty looked in her purse. All she had left was $1.75. If only she hadn't bought the brooch.

"You got a car?" asked the man. "Where'll I take it?"

"I'm walking," said Letty. "I'll carry it."

The man laughed as if it was a big joke.

"Carry it?" he cried. "A skinny little kid like you?"

Now he was more friendly.

"I'll tell you what I'll do," he said. He found a nice tree for her. "This one's a little lopsided, but you can have it for one fifty. That'll leave you twenty-five cents for a taxi. Here's a taxi now."

A man got out of the taxi and Letty got in with her tree. The man called "Merry Christmas" after her. The taxi driver took her and the tree home for twenty-five cents.

It was nearly dark when she got there. Days were short now in December, and night clamped down early. The three dogs were on the porch as usual, Trixie, Patches, and Jerry. They slept on the porch to keep burglars away.

Now they thought Letty was a burglar. They barked and barked as she came up, pulling the tree behind her. Now everybody would see it. Letty had hoped supper would be over and Punky and Mike in bed and, of course, Dad not home yet. Dad was not coming home for Christmas! She wanted to set the tree up in the front room and surprise them all.

But they were all there eating supper—Aunt Vi, too, of course not Dad. Punky had fallen asleep on the couch. Mom called to Letty but Letty was too excited now to eat supper. She put up the tree all by herself. She found Dad's hammer and fixed a brace at the bottom to keep it from falling over. She found the lights and the cord and put them on. She tied the shiny balls on. She turned the switch and the tree looked beautiful.

Then Punky woke up. How surprised she was to see a tree with lights on it! On Christmas Eve, too!

Punky danced around the tree and tripped over the light cord. She grabbed the cord and pulled it. The lights went out. Punky pulled the colored balls off. She dropped one of them and broke it.

Letty took Punky and spanked her.

She plugged the cord in again and put the balls back on.

At least it was something for Christmas.

Letty was tired now and felt like going to bed. She reached for a hot dog off the table and gulped it down. It was all she wanted to eat. She wasn't hungry.

She and Mike looked at each other. They looked round the house. There were no signs of Christmas—except the tree.

"I paid all my baby-sitting money for it!" Letty bragged.

Mom scolded. "You were saving for a new coat. You need a coat more than we need a tree."

Letty turned to Mike. "Tomorrow's Christmas. No presents anywhere. Didn't I tell you?" she whispered.

It was in the middle of the night when Daddy came and wakened them. That is, it seemed like the middle of the night. It was really six in the morning.

"Merry Christmas! Merry Christmas!" shouted Daddy. When did he come? How did he get there? Did he get an unexpected day off?

Dad was wheeling a bike. Where had it come from?

"But, Mom!" cried Letty. She rubbed her eyes as if she'd been dreaming: "You said there was no money..."

Mike was so happy, he did not ask where the bike came from. He did not notice that it was scuffed and secondhand. It was a bike at last.

Mom was opening a big box beside her. She took a small one out and handed it to Letty. Letty opened it. There lay a wristwatch—a real one, not a Mickey Mouse one. Letty could not believe her eyes.

"So you won't miss the school bus," said Mom.

Letty threw her arms around Mom's neck. Then she hugged Dad.

"You are both FAKES!" she cried. "Mom said there was no money ... and that Dad couldn't get home..."

Best of all was Punky's doll. It had blue eyes that closed, yellow curls, and white teeth. It was as big as a baby, as big as Punky could hold. She walked up and down, patting the doll and singing to it.

Letty plugged in the lights on the tree. Dad stared. "Where on earth did *that* come from?"

Letty still could not understand. She looked from Mom to Dad. How did they find out about the bike and the watch and the doll? She forgot that she and Mike and Punky had been talking about what they wanted for weeks in advance.

Mike had the answer.

"Santa Claus brought them," he said.

Suddenly Letty thought of something. She ran into the bedroom and came out with a little box. She took out the beautiful butterfly brooch. She had wanted it for herself, but now it was Christmas, so she knew what she wanted to do. She'd give it to Mom.

She turned to Mom and pinned it on her shoulder.

"Merry Christmas, Mom!" she said.

"What! For *me*?" cried Mom.

Mom kissed her and they all said, "Merry Christmas!"

Christmas Tree So Green

Christmas tree so green,
    With lights of red and blue,
How many hours of happiness
    Can we ever give to you?

Christmas tree so green,
    Do you remember where
You grew upon the hillside
    Out in the sun and air?

Christmas tree so green,
    Are you sad to be away
From the snakes, the quails, the rabbits,
    And the birds that sang all day?

Christmas tree so green,
    Do you miss the summer sun,
And the rain and snow that soaked you
    Until the storm was done?

Christmas tree so sad,
    Your homesickness unseen,
Is that why now indoors
    You drop your needles green?

BEFORE SNOW FLIES

A Tree-Farm Christmas

WHERE do all of our Christmas trees come from? So many hundreds of thousands of trees are cut and used for decoration each year. If they were all taken from our forests, our tree supply would soon be depleted. Instead, they come from tree farms, where Christmas trees are specially grown from seed, tenderly and scientifically cared for, and then marketed for the Christmas trade. Tree farms are located in various parts of our country—Montana, Michigan, New England, Canada, and other places.

The Dirkson family lived in Muskegon, Michigan. Their entire living depended on the Christmas trees they grew on a farm twelve miles out from town, which, because of its sandy soil, Mother called Sahara. With them, growing Christmas trees was a family affair. Although the Dirkson children were all girls—Susan, Amy, Ruth, and Betty, they helped their parents with all the work and enjoyed it. They helped plant trees, prune them, weed them, tag them, pile them, and load the cut trees on the truck. Getting the trees out was the biggest job of all.

"Hurry! Hurry!" called Mother. "Let's get started."
Mother loaded the car. She thought of all the things they might

need—hot food and drinks, extra clothing, gloves, overshoes and blankets, cans of Bab-O, twine and rope, Daddy's saw, the old baby carriage, and all the boxes of tags.

The fall was the busy time of year. Getting the Christmas trees out was a family affair. Every weekend in October they had been going to Sahara. The trees had to be cut before Thanksgiving. Orders had come in through the summer and now they must be filled.

Before snow flies! Before snow flies! The children heard Mother say it over and over.

There was work for every one.

Before the trees were cut, they had to be tagged. That was a job for Mother and the girls. The body had been taken off of the frame of the baby carriage, and a flat top put on. This held the cigar boxes full of tags of different colors—blue, yellow, red, and white. Each tag had a number marked on it. Red 7, Blue 5, indicating the height of a tree in feet. Each color meant a certain buyer. Some buyers wanted stiff needles, or a certain shape or size.

LOIS LENSKI

Daddy measured the trees and kept his yardstick in the crook of a tree when not in use. He tried to give each customer just what he asked for.

Little Betty and Ruth pushed the cart.

Mother, Susan, and Amy tied the tags on. They walked along and tagged and tagged and tagged.

After the trees were tagged, Daddy sawed the trees down with a special saw. Susan was right there to catch each tree as it fell. Then the trees had to be dragged to piles in the fire lane.

"Get hold of the butt," called Susan, "not the top!" Betty and Ruth were trying to help. "Don't take such big ones, take the little ones."

The children all wore wool gloves to keep the pitch pine and tar off their hands.

Amy and Susan dragged the bigger trees to the piles. They would lie there until almost Thanksgiving time.

"But, Daddy," said Susan, "won't the tree-rustlers come and steal them?"

Mother was anxious, too. "How can we hide them?" she asked.

"We'll pile them behind that multiflora rose hedge," said Daddy.

"And stand a row up in front to hide the butts. Then they can't be seen from the road."

Mother did the piling. All the butt ends had to point the same way. She packed them soldily, one on top of the other.

"Won't they get wilted?" asked Susan. "It's a long time until Christmas."

"They'll be fine, if kept out in the cold," said Mother. "Scotch pine will stay fresh all winter out of doors, better than spruce or fir. If there's a warm spell, we many have some losses. Just so we get them all cut and piled before snow and ice come."

"Mother, I've got poison ivy again," said Susan.

She rolled up her jacket sleeve. There were red spots on her arms.

"There's no poison ivy now," said Mother. "It was all killed by the frost."

"I've got measles, then! Please look!" insisted Susan.

Mother looked. "The trees prick, just like measles," she said. "It's not serious."

"But it prickles!"

Ruth and Betty laughed. "We prickle, too!" they said.

At noon the family rested and ate lunch sitting in the back of the truck. They had boxes for tables and wool blankets to hang over the sides to keep the cold wind out. Everybody was hungry and the food tasted good. As it was dangerous to make a fire, because of the trees, Mother always brought hot food along. Today she had spaghetti and meat balls, fruit, and cookies.

"Now, back to work!" called Mother. "Daddy wants to get the truck loaded, so he can go to Chicago tomorrow."

"I'm going with him," said Susan. "Daddy said I could."

"It's a long hard ride," said Mother. "Are you sure you want to go?"

Susan was very sure. Amy went the last time. Now it was Susan's turn. After the trees were sold, Daddy would pay her.

All afternoon they loaded the truck. Susan loved this part, although it was hard work. She stood on the hood of the truck. Mother handed a tree to her, and she handed it to Daddy. Daddy stood in the body of the truck to pack the trees. They had to be loaded carefully to keep from breaking branches off.

The trees were piled twice as high as the cab, their butt ends sticking out back and sides. Now Susan had to stand on the top of the cab and Amy on the hood. The girls tried to throw small trees up, but it was too hard. So Mother did it for them. Daddy nested the small trees inside the big ones. The Chicago order was for all sizes.

As the load got higher, the trees got heavier and heavier to lift. Everybody's arms began to ache.

Daddy was down in the middle packing. Whew! Here came a big tree over his head.

"Watch out, Daddy! We'll hit you!" cried Susan.

Daddy climbed out and filled the hole up with trees.

"Gosh!" he cried. "I've lost one overshoe! It must be buried down under the trees!"

"And I've lost my glove!" cried Susan. "My hands are getting cold."

Mother brought out an extra overshoe and glove from her emergency supply.

A north wind had blown up, and all the faces were rosy with cold. Ruth and Betty began to sniffle.

"Let's go home!" they wailed.

But they could not stop until the truck was loaded. At last Daddy climbed down, and tied the load to the truck with strong, half-inch rope.

"It must be tight for the trip to Chicago," he said. "I don't want to lose half my trees on the highway."

It was dark when they started at six A.M. And snowing, but the snow stopped before they had gone very far.

Mother gave them fruit and sandwiches to eat along the way. When they stopped at a gas station, Daddy bought Susan a Coke and candy bars.

Susan never realized before how far it was to Chicago. She had been there a number of times to visit Grandma Dirkson. But they had always driven in the car. This was her first trip in the truck. She thought they would never get there.

LOIS LENSKI

The load was for several florists on the West Side in the Sunset Hills suburb. They wanted the trees for *flocking*. Daddy explained.

"They blow in shredded plastic with one machine," he said, "and glue with another. The plastic is white or pink or any color they want. They like Scotch pine for this better than spruce or balsam, as the pine does not drop its needles."

But Susan had dozed off and hardly heard him. She slept at Grandma Dirkson's that night and rested all the next day. It was good to visit with Grandma. Grandma understood about the horse she wanted. Grandma hoped they would soon get their home in the country.

The next day, they started back to Muskegon. The truck was empty now, and it bounced and bumped along the highway. So many cars and trucks were coming and going, it made Susan dizzy. Suddenly she felt sick at her stomach. Daddy looked at her and her face was white.

He pulled up at the next gas station and got her some ginger ale. She rested awhile, then they went on again. Daddy said it was three hundred and sixty miles round trip.

Susan was glad to get home that night. She went right to bed tucking her purse under her pillow. The purse was full of money—more than she had ever had before. Sick as she was, she smiled to herself.

She had worked hard and earned it all.

She would get her horse at last.

"Our blue spruces weren't stolen, after all!" Daddy said.

"No?" Mother looked surprised.

"All that trouble I took to find the thieves," Daddy said, "went for nothing."

"What do you mean?" asked Mother.

"I got it all cleared up in Chicago," said Daddy. "The company in Chicago sent a new man out and he came to the wrong tree farm. Hofstad had sold them *his* spruces, and the man took *mine* by mistake! But I got my money all right!"

"Good!" said Mother.

The day after he returned from Chicago, Daddy had a busy time. Three buyers came to look his plantings over. They liked his trees and gave large orders.

The next week was busier than ever, as Daddy worked to get orders out. Rob Wilson and another young man worked all week long.

A neighbor, Vic Carlson, came over to help.

The orders were so large, the company sent a big semitruck to pick up the trees. The truck was too large to go into the field. so after loading Daddy's small truck in the lane, Mother had to drive it out to the road. There the men reloaded the trees onto the semi. Some of the orders were for big red pines. Their limbs had to be drawn up and tied tightly to the trunk with binder's twine for easier packing and less breakage. The Scotch pines did not have to be tied.

On the weekend Mother and the girls came out to help in the field. After the trees were cut, they dragged them into the fire lanes and piled them up in piles, their butt ends pointing all the same way.

They all worked together. After a while, Susan went off alone up the slope to the end of the row. She stopped there to look at the view. Acres and acres that had been useless sand-blown land were now covered with beautiful trees. She could see the Hofstad farm, and another farmhouse, old and empty, standing near. She began to dream . . .

But a rustling noise caught her ear.

What was it? A possum? A deer? A snake? Snakes made no noise, deer did not come out until night . . . She turned quickly. There behind a tall red pine she saw it. The bear—Susan's bear!

She held her breath, as she watched. He did not notice her. He was going his own way. What big arms he had! Yes, his arms were bigger than Daddy's. Where did he live? Where was he going? Was he looking for a hole to sleep in all winter?

She watched until he was out of sight. Then she ran back to the others. Amy laughed when she told about it. The little girls were frightened and wanted to go home.

"Susan's bear!" teased Amy. "Susan's always seeing bears!"

"But I did see him, Mother!" cried Susan. "Make Amy stop teasing me."

Mother turned to Amy. "That's enough," she said. Then she put her arm around Susan's shoulders.

"I believe you, dear," Mother said. "I saw the bear myself!"

Amy gasped. "You did? Why didn't you tell us?"

"I didn't want to scare you," said Mother. "And I didn't want to scare the bear either. He was doing no harm. I thought it best to just let him go."

The weeks, so filled with work, passed all to quickly.

At last it was Christmas and time to go to Grandma Dirkson's in Chicago. Mother loaded the car with suitcases, boxes of food, and gift packages. It wouldn't be Christmas without spending three or four days at Grandma's. It was snowing hard. Everybody liked snow for Christmas.

The highways were plowed clear and the ice melted at midday. The trip seemed much shorter in the car than in the truck, and Susan did not get sick at all.

Christmas Day was wonderful—church and dinner and lovely gifts for everybody. This year there were two surprises. Daddy announced the first.

"We've waited a long time *for our trees to come in*," he said. "This year we've seen hundreds of them *go out*. So it's beginning to pay off. I'm glad to say that right here I have a Christmas gift for us all." He opened a large envelope and took out a folded paper.

"This is the deed to our new home! We've bought the old farm by the Hofstads! It joins our Sahara acreage. As soon as we remodel the house, we'll move out to the country! We'll be nearer to our trees and can take better care of them."

They all cheered, but Susan could not speak. She ran to Daddy and put her arms tightly around him. Then she showed him one of her gifts.

"Look what Grandma gave me," she said.

She opened a red leather purse and began counting the dollar bills inside. She read the card that came with the purse: "A horse for Christmas! Grandma wants to help a hard-working little girl."

"With the money I earned and all this from Grandma—will it be enough?" Susan asked.

"I think so," said Daddy. "Hofstad wants you to have the horse. He'll take care of it till we move out to the country."

Susan ran to Grandma and gave her a big hug.

"There's a barn on the farm," said Daddy.

"A good home for Wildfire," said Susan.

Then they all bundled up, got in Daddy's car and went for a ride. It was cold and had started to snow again. Through the curved and winding streets of Sunset Hills they drove, to look at the Christmas decorations. In the big picture windows of the lovely homes, they saw Christmas trees, some green, some white or colored. They were trimmed with big red bows and just a few big red glass balls.

"*Our* trees!" said Amy.

"*Our* trees!" said Betty and Ruth.

"*Our* trees!" said Mother and Daddy. "They've made so many people happy."

"*Our* trees!" said Susan. "With an angel on top!"

The Star

The leaves are gone,
     The trees are bare;
The wind blows cold—
     No flowers fair.

No garden now,
     Not even weeds;
No squirrel to jump
     And look for seeds.

No bird to chirp
     And sing all day;
No turtle walks,
     No worm to play.

Above the roofs,
     No sign of light;
The sky is black,
     As black as night.

And then it comes
     The star! Afar!
Up there it shines
     The first bright star!

THE FIRST STAR

A Polish Christmas

How STRANGE in a huge, bustling city, filled with tall buildings, crowded with shops, offices, and factories, and noisy with heavy traffic, to suddenly come upon a quiet village in its very heart! A quiet village, with rows of small two-story houses, set in yards with green grass and beds of blooming flowers. A quiet village, where it is safe for children to play in yard or alley, where women hang their washing on clotheslines in the back yard to dry and smell sweet in the warm sun! A quiet village, where church steeples tower over little houses, and where men, women, and children go in and out on Sundays and weekdays, saying their prayers, singing hymns of praise, and thanking the Lord for His manifold blessings.

Such is the village of Hamtramck, in the very heart of the big city of Detroit. Here Polish people came after the beginning of the century, to make their homes; the men to work in the nearby automobile plants and the women to care for their homes and families, both indulging in their love of the good earth by surrounding themselves with flowers and vegetables and all manner of growing things, tended by their own hands with loving care.

Here Polish families bring up their children and perpetuate many of their Old-World Polish customs, accommodating them, to a certain extent, to American ones. Christmas has always been a deeply-felt religious festival to the Polish people and still remains so. Every family makes elaborate preparations for it—many Polish women insist on repainting their entire houses themselves. Nothing is too good for Christmas.

The Baroszewicz family was much like the others. Dad worked at the Dodge plant, and the children, Josef, Tekla, and Marya, often drove in the car with Mom to pick him up after work and bring him home. Uncle Chris and Aunt Bertha ran the Polka Bakery, baking all the delicious baked goods that they sold there. Uncle Chris's specialty was cherry pies—no one could match those that came from his oven.

The children made up most of the games that they played in the yard after school with the neighbor children. Dad had had a layoff and was eager to get back to work again. Mom started to paint the kitchen, fell off the ladder and broke her ankle. Fall turned into winter, and soon the Polish people began to think about Christmas. Soon it was time for the annual party at the Dodge plant.

Open House at the Dodge plant was fun for everybody. Even Grandma and Grandpa went. The auto plant looked quite festive with its fresh paint and bouquets of flowers. Delicious refreshments were served, punch, and many kinds of Polish cakes.

All the neighbors were there. It was fun to see them even if they lived right down the street or across the alley. Old Lady Rukse was there and she and Grandma found chairs and visited.

Mom was able to walk now, using her walker. She laughed as she told people about falling off the ladder.

"I'm dying to pick up a paint brush again!" she said.

The kitchen did not get painted until just before Christmas. And what a happy time that was! Josef was always glad to be Polish, and especially so at Christmas time. The old-country customs made life in America so much richer.

On Christmas Eve, Tekla and Marya sat on the back steps and waited. The leaves were off the trees now, and it was cold. All of Grandma's beautiful flowers were gone. There were no birds or squirrels in the pear tree. The sky grew darker and darker over the tops of the houses that lined the back alley.

Then at last they saw it.

"The star! The first star!" cried little Marya.

They ran into the house and told the news. The first star was the sign for the Vigil Supper to begin.

Everybody was there, and everything was ready. The Christmas tree was trimmed and gifts covered the floor beneath it. They all took their places at the long dining table. An empty place was set for a stranger, in memory of the dead.

Grandpa, at the head of the table, broke the large Christmas wafer and one by one, shared it with the others. He wished them health and happiness. Then the feast began, with twelve meatless dishes. At midnight, the whole family went to Christmas Eve Mass at the great church on the corner.

Merry Christmas! Merry Christmas!

It was truly a merry Christmas for the Baroszewicz family. Mom was well, Dad was back at work, Uncle Eddie had a job, and everyone was happy.

Christt Child Small

What shall we give Thee,
      Christ child small?
Give Thee nothing
      Or give Thee all?

What shall we give Thee?
      Flowers so sweet—
None are too lovely
      Our Guest to greet.

What shall we give Thee,
      Silver and gold?
Or all of the riches
      The world can hold?

What shall we give Thee,
      Christ child small?
The love in our hearts—
      It is our all.

VISIT OF THE SHEPHERDS

A Nativity Play

SCENE I

Shepherds on Hillside

(MODERN BOY *and* GIRL *enter. They see* SHEPHERDS *stretched out asleep*)

BOY: Look! There are people, asleep on the hillside.

GIRL: I see some sheep. They must be shepherds.

BOY: I thought they had to stay awake all night to protect their sheep.

GIRL: At night is when the wolves come—to steal the lambs away.

(*A bright light comes into the blue sky above the sleeping figures. It gets brighter and brighter. It flickers off and on*)

BOY: Look! They're stirring.

GIRL: They're waking up. The starlight is so bright.

BOY: It's shining in their eyes. I can't sleep with a light shining in my eyes either.

GIRL: I always close my bedroom door. Look! They're talking.

BOY: They're scared of something.
GIRL: Oh, look!
BOY: Sh! Let's listen . . .
(CHORUS OF CHILDREN *comes softly on stage at back*)
(SHEPHERDS *waking and stretching*)
1ST SHEPHERD: The stars are so bright—
      Have I slept all night?
      Did I hear a song?
      Is anything wrong?

2ND SHEPHERD: I am stiff with cold,
      My knees bend and fold!
      I can hardly walk—
      I'm too sleepy to talk.

3RD SHEPHERD: Now it's dry, now it's wet,
      How bedraggled we get;
      Now it's snow, now it's sleet,
      Shoes freeze to our feet.

1ST SHEPHERD: A hard life, I agree,
      Silly shepherds do we be.
      But—what comes to my ear?
      Is it music I hear?

(Chorus *sings: The Angels' Song*)

  Glory to God in the highest,
   Glory to God, they sang;
  Glory to God in the highest,
   The song of the angels rang.

   Peace on earth,
   To men good will;

Peace on earth—
We sing it still.

Glory to God in the highest,
Glory to God, they sang;
Glory to God in the highest,
The song of the angels rang.

BOY: Peace on earth . . . to men good will . . .
GIRL: Peace on earth . . . we sing it still.
BOY: But we don't put it in practice.
GIRL: We ought to try harder.
BOY: We ought to stop quarreling and fighting. That's peace.
GIRL: We ought to like people more. That's good will.
(ANGEL GABRIEL *steps apart and announces:*)
Wake up now!
No time for sleep!
Go—leave your flocks,
Your hills, your sheep.

Do not delay,
Go find your way—
God's son is born
This very morn.

The greatest wonder
On this earth,
Go—witness now—
The Christ child's birth.

(CHORUS *goes out, singing:* "Glory to God in the highest . . ." *softly*)
(*Star moves slowly from R to L*)
1ST SHEPHERD: The star is moving. Let's follow it.
2ND SHEPHERD: Let's go see what this is all about.
3RD SHEPHERD: I don't want to miss anything. I like to see everything
that goes on.

4TH SHEPHERD: Let's eat first. I'm hungry. No telling when we'll get back.

1ST SHEPHERD: You're always hungry. But—maybe we'd better eat.
(They sit down in a group)

2ND SHEPHERD: Pass me the headcheese.

3RD SHEPHERD: I like black bread. I could eat it all day.

4TH SHEPHERD: Onions and headcheese on the black bread. That's what I call good.

(They eat greedily)

1ST SHEPHERD: Hey! The star's moving. If we're gonna follow, we better get a move on.

2ND SHEPHERD: The star will wait for us. It will show us the way.

3RD SHEPHERD: How do you know it will wait? If the light goes out, we'll get lost in the dark.

4TH SHEPHERD: Another piece of black bread. I'm not through eating.

3RD SHEPHERD: Here it is now. Make haste. Gobble it up quick.

1ST SHEPHERD: I'll take my sheepskin along. The night is cold.

2ND SHEPHERD: I'll take these sticks of wood. We might need a fire.

3RD SHEPHERD: You can never tell what you'll need when you go on a journey. I'll take my water jug. We'll need a drink sure.

4TH SHEPHERD: Here's our last loaf of black bread. We'll need bread to eat. I'll take it along.

(They bustle about, making preparations)

1ST SHEPHERD: Come on, let's go.

5TH SHEPHERD: *(all this time asleep, now wakes up)* : Where are you going, anyhow? *(They do not answer)* All right, go on then. I'm too sleepy. I'll stay here. I was up late last night.

2ND SHEPHERD: Sleep on now and take your rest. But sleep with one eye and one ear open. Be sure to wake up when the wolf howls. Keep him away from the lambs.

3RD SHEPHERD: *(looking back)* : You're just too lazy to go. But somebody has to stay and look after the sheep.

5TH SHEPHERD: Go on! Be off! I'm glad to see the last of you!

(He curls up and goes to sleep again. Starts snoring. The first four go off left, looking up at the star)

(2ND SHEPHERD *lingers behind the others. Looks scared and bewildered*)

BOY: What's the matter, shepherd? Are you lost?

2ND SHEPHERD: I've been going in circles. Will I ever catch up with
them?

GIRL: They went that way. (*points*) The star moved that way. Follow
the star.

(BOY *and* 2ND SHEPHERD *sing dialogue song: Shepherd, Lonely Shepherd*)

BOY: Shepherd, lonely shepherd,
Why are you afraid?

SHEPHERD: I heard the song of the angels,
In shining light arrayed.

BOY: Shepherd, lonely shepherd.
Why do you leave your sheep?

SHEPHERD: I go to find a holy Babe,
In a stable fast asleep.

BOY: Shepherd, lonely shepherd,
Whom do you wish to greet?

SHEPHERD: I go to find my blessed King,
To worship at His feet.

(*Curtain*)

SCENE II

Before the Inn

(Inn *on R, with door and lighted window, and sign above. Barn on*
L; *wall between. L side is kept dark. Star shines out above darkened barn*)
(BOY *and* GIRL *come in on L; four* SHEPHERDS *on R*)

1ST SHEPHERD: This must be the place.

2ND SHEPHERD: The star stands still.

3RD SHEPHERD: It's as bright as ever.

4TH SHEPHERD (*studying Inn sign*): What does it say: I N N—what
does that spell? Two N's—does that spell RUN? Let's
RUN then.

3RD SHEPHERD: It spells INN, not RUN, stupid.

4TH SHEPHERD: If it spells INN, it must be an INN, so we better go
IN—or else RUN as fast as we KIN!

(*The others get excited and nervous*)

BOY (*stepping forward*): I hope you brought your gifts for the Christ
child.

GIRL (*in a somewhat bossy tone*): Get them all ready before you go in.

1ST SHEPHERD: Gifts? What do you mean?

GIRL: Presents. Aren't you going to give the Baby Jesus something?

2ND SHEPHERD: Sure. We brought presents.

1ST SHEPHERD: I brought my sheepskin.

2ND SHEPHERD: I brought my sticks of wood.

3RD SHEPHERD: I brought my water jug.

4TH SHEPHERD: I brought my black bread. (*Takes loaf out of his pocket, and starts to bite off one end*)

BOY (*in shocked tone*) : Not *those* kind of presents!

GIRL: *Such* presents for a baby! If I went to see the Baby Jesus, I'd give him . . . (*looks about on her person*) I'd give him . . . (*holds up her arm so all can see it*) my *gold wristwatch!*

SHEPHERDS (*ashamed, looking down at their gifts*) : It's all we have.

BOY: Poor fellows. They haven't got anything else to give.

GIRL (*impatiently*) : Well! Aren't you going in? What are we waiting for?

1ST SHEPHERD: This must be the place all right. (*turns to* 2ND SHEPHERD) You go and knock at the door.

2ND SHEPHERD: No. I'm scared. *You* go. (*turns to* 3RD SHEPHERD)

3RD SHEPHERD (*quavering voice*) : Oh, no! Not me! My knees are shaking. I'm shaking all over. *You* go. (*turns to* 4TH SHEPHERD)

4TH SHEPHERD: No sir-ree. I wish I'd never come. I wish I had stayed out on the hillside to watch the sheep. I don't like towns and bright lights . . . and so many people.

1ST SHEPHERD: I s'pose *I'll* have to, then.

(*He creeps up to Inn door and knocks timidly*)

BOY: Nobody will hear that. They're eating and drinking in there.

GIRL: You'll have to knock louder. Can't you hear them laughing inside?

BOY: You'll have to rattle the latch.

GIRL: You'll have to pound on the door.

1ST SHEPHERD: Louder, then. (*summons his courage and knocks very loudly. The door opens with a jerk and cross* INNKEEPER *puts his head out, shouting*)

INNKEEPER: No room! NO ROOM AT THE INN, I SAID! How many times do I have to tell you? Be off now, or I'll kick you on the shins!

(INNKEEPER *sings: No Room at the Inn*)

> No room at the inn,
> No room, I said!
> To travelers all,
> I offer no bed.

No room at the inn,
I see no star;
I do not care
How tired they are.

No room at the inn,
I close my door;
I said, Be off,
And knock no more.

(CHORUS OF CHILDREN *sing fourth verse, softly, as if in echo*) :

O Lord, may I not
Send Thee away;
There's room in my heart
For Thee to stay.

(INNKEEPER *looks down, sees trembling shepherd*)

INNKEEPER: Oh! You're somebody else. I told that man and woman there was no room at the inn. I told them they could sleep in the barn. I felt sorry for the woman—the night was so cold. But—who are *you*? What do you *want*?

1ST SHEPHERD: Where did they go?

INNKEEPER: The man and woman? Are you looking for them? In the barn, I suppose. How should I know where they went? I can't keep an eye on everybody. I've got important things to attend to. (*closes door sharply*)

(1ST SHEPHERD *comes back to group on R*)

1ST SHEPHERD: You heard what he said.

OTHERS: Yes, we heard. (*shaking heads*) He wasn't very friendly. He didn't make us very welcome.

4TH SHEPHERD: I'm going back to the hillside, to help . . . with the sheep.

2ND SHEPHERD: No, wait. We're going in. This is what we came for.

BOY: You'd better wait. If you go, you'll be sorry.

GIRL (*excitedly*) : Oh! Just look who's coming! (*looking off-stage R*)

BOY (*eagerly*) : They look like KINGS!

GIRL (*clapping her hands*) : I just adore KINGS and QUEENS. Oh, see their colorful robes, their gold, and their jewels. This is something like it!

(*The* THREE KINGS *enter slowly from R, pointing to star, one behind the other, walking slowly.* CHORUS OF CHILDREN *appears backstage, between inn and barn.* CHORUS *sings: A Greater King Than They*)

> *The first king was tall*
> *And dressed in red;*
> *He wore a crown*
> *Upon his head.*
>
> *The next king was short*
> *And dressed in blue;*
> *His crown of gold*
> *Was jeweled too.*
>
> *The third king came next—*
> *Not short nor tall;*
> *A purple robe*
> *At his feet did fall.*
>
> *Gold, frankincense, and myrrh brought they,*
> *Watching the star that pointed the way;*
> *They brought their gifts*
> *To the Babe on the hay,*
> *For they knew He was*
> *A greater King than they.*

(KINGS *go off L, as if going into barn*)

(SHEPHERDS *in a huddle on R, begin to speak*)

1ST SHEPHERD: That was *our* star.

2ND SHEPHERD: We saw it first.

3RD SHEPHERD: They had no business coming here. They were just showing off.

4TH SHEPHERD: Too many people in these towns. I like it better out on the hillside.

BOY (*ignoring shepherds*): I just love parades.

GIRL: They should have had a band.

BOY (*Looks at shepherds, as if surprised to find them still there*): The three kings are gone now. It's your turn to go in.

1ST SHEPHERD: By rights we should have gone in first.

2ND SHEPHERD (*whimpering*): I'm afraid of that mean old Innkeeper.

3RD SHEPHERD: He said he'd kick us on the shins.

(*One pushes the other:*) You go. No, you go. You go first. I'll follow you.

(*Timidly, one opens the barn door. A double screen opens and reveals the manger scene, with Mary, Joseph, and the baby in manger. The gold gifts left by the kings may be seen in front. The star moves down closer and lights up the scene. The CHORUS OF CHILDREN stands silent behind the manger group*)

1ST SHEPHERD (*kneels and offers sheepskin*): He must be cold.

2ND SHEPHERD (*lays wood for fire*): I'll make a fire for Him.

3RD SHEPHERD (*offers water jug*): Water is good when you're thirsty.

4TH SHEPHERD (*offers loaf of bread*): Bread tastes sweet when you're hungry.

(CHORUS *sings: O Babe in the Manger*)

> *O Babe in the manger,*
>   *We come to Thee;*
> *We bring our gift*
>   *On bended knee.*
>
> *Our gifts so unworthy,*
>   *Our courage small,*
> *Our footsteps slow—*
>   *O bless us all.*
>
> *Thou, Babe in the manger,*
>   *Teach us, we pray,*
> *To love, to live*
>   *With Thee each day.*

(*A motley array of people crowd in on the right, dressed to represent different trades and occupations, as if Bethlehem townspeople*)

ONE *says*: We heard there was a KING here. Where is he?

ANOTHER *says*: We saw the bright light made by the star. What was that for?

4TH SHEPHERD (*turns to go*): Too many people. Where did all these people come from? I can't stand so many people. Come, let's go back to the hillside.

1ST, 2ND, 3RD SHEPHERDS: Yes, we have seen Him. Come, let's go.

(*All four go out together, singing: Long Will We Remember*)

> Long will we remember the baby King;
> Ne'er will we forget the song the angels sing;
> In the dark nights on the hillside,
> In the starlight,
> In the snow,
> With our flocks that wander restless,
> As we follow where they go—
> May we keep our vision clear,
> May we keep the Christ child near.

BOY (*to people crowding in*): WHO ARE YOU? What do you people want?

GIRL: Stop pushing! You have no business here. You were not invited.

A COBBLER: I am a cobbler. I made Him some shoes.

A TINSMITH: I am a tinsmith. I made Him a plate and cup.

A WEAVER: I am a weaver. I wove Him a suit of clothes.

A CARPENTER: I am a carpenter. I made Him a table and a chair.

GIRL: Whatever does a baby want with things like *that*?

BOY: Just stop and think a minute. He'll soon grow up and have use for them. That's all they have to give.

(CHORUS *sings: It's All We Have to Give. Crowd of people join in on second verse:*)

It's all we have to give—
  The love in our hearts,
  The work of our hands—
That's all we have to give.

We bring our love to Thee,
  We love with our heart,
  We work with our hands—
We bring it now to Thee.

(Manger scene darkens. People put their arms around each other in friendship. They sing:)

              Glory to God in the highest,
                Glory to God, they sang;
              Glory to God in the highest,
                The song of the angels rang.
Boy *sings, solo:*   *Peace on earth*
                To men good will;
Girl *sings, solo:*   *Peace on earth—*
                We sing it still.
All together sing: *Glory to God in the highest,*
              The song of the angels rang.
                    (Curtain)
                    The End